SHAD[illegible] THE PAST

AN ARLA BAKER MYSTERY

BOOK 15

M.L. ROSE

CHAPTER 1

Martin Keane had lived on the Regent's Canal for twelve years, but he'd never seen the water this low. The drought had transformed the familiar waterway into something alien – a deep groove of exposed brick and centuries of London muck. His narrowboat, *The Borrowed Time,* sat awkwardly in the shallow water, listing slightly to port.

The morning had dawned warm and bright, the kind of July day that already felt suffused with warmth. Martin stood on the towpath, surveying the debris that the receding water had revealed. Most of the canal's secrets were predictably mundane: shopping trolleys, bicycles, the usual urban detritus. But something about the way the morning light caught a patch of dark material under the footbridge made him pause.

He'd been meaning to clear some of the rubbish while the water was low enough to reach it. Environmental responsibility was part of the unofficial narrowboat owners' code, though most treated it more as a guideline than a rule. Martin took it seriously. He'd spent his career as a geography teacher before retiring; environmental consciousness was hard-wired into him now.

The material that had caught his eye was half-buried in the slick mud of the canal bed, about six feet from where he stood. It looked like tarpaulin, the heavy-duty kind used to cover boats and scaffolding in building sites. Probably another bit of rubbish to add to his collection. He grabbed his extending rubbish picker and wellies from *The Borrowed Time's* rear deck.

"Going treasure hunting?" Carol from the boat next door called out. She was on her deck with her morning coffee, wrapped in a flowery robe, equally flowery cardigan and slacks underneath.

"Someone has to clean up after the lovely citizens of London," Martin replied, pulling on his wellies. "Want to place bets on what I'll find? My money's on at least three phones and someone's lost house keys."

"Tenner says you find gold nuggets," Carol laughed, raising her coffee mug in a salute.

Martin carefully picked his way down the sloping canal bank. The drought had exposed about four feet of the usually submerged wall, creating a treacherous muddy slope. The mud sucked at his boots, releasing a ripe organic smell that made him wish he'd brought a mask.

The tarpaulin was more firmly wedged than he'd expected. He gave it an experimental tug with the litter picker, but it barely moved. Something heavy was keeping it in place. Martin crouched down, trying to get a better angle. The material was degraded, splitting apart in places. Through one of the larger tears, he could see something pale beneath.

It was smooth, pale yellow, almost shiny, as if it had been preserved carefully.

His mind cycled through several possibilities – a shop mannequin, a plastic garden statue, a large doll? But what would any of that be doing in a tarp covering, at the bottom of a canal?

He tugged harder, and the rattling material inside shifted, and then slid further down the bank.

Then breath caught in his chest, and he felt the sudden constriction of fear. His head jerked back as he tried to get a better look.

The curved shape, yellowed with age but unmistakable in its anatomical accuracy, was a human skull. The skull was still attached to the spine, and the ribs spread out from it, the rest of the skeleton hidden from view. It was human, there was no doubt.

He reminded himself to breathe, but his chest was tighter than when he had a heart attack, five years ago. His eyes closed, and he breathed deeply, slowly. He needed to stay in control. He straightened up carefully, mindful of disturbing nothing.

"Carol," he called, keeping his voice steady. "Could you bring me your phone? And you might want to call 999 while you're at it."

Carol must have heard something in his tone because she didn't ask questions. A moment later, she was picking her way down the bank, phone in hand like it was a weapon, and she was coming to save Martin.

She stood next to him, and her gasp, and the way her hand covered her mouth was proof enough she had seen what he had.

It was real. She turned her back to the tarp bag and its grisly contents, and Martin raised a hand to her shoulders. They stood like that for a while, mute in the sunshine.

“Give me the phone,” Martin rasped hoarsely.

"Police, please," he said, when connected to 999. "Yes, we've found something in the canal. Human remains, we think." Another pause. "Regent's Canal, just by the Prince Albert Bridge in Camden. Near the lock."

Martin stood guard over his discovery, watching the morning light strengthen. Dog walkers and joggers were starting to appear on the towpath. A few slowed down to look curiously at him and Carol, but most carried on with their routines, unaware of the canal's gruesome secret.

CHAPTER 2

DCI Arla Baker was in the driver's seat of her VW Golf, watching Nicole as the teenager examined herself in the mirror. Then she flipped up the sun cover and glanced at her mother.

"Bye mum. See you later."

Arla couldn't help but think how much Nicole had changed in the last three years. She was a completely different child from when she was ten. She was taller now, and when she wore jeans, she looked scarily mature. Like all parents, Arla was loving the transition, but a part of her pined for her little girl, the one who ran round the garden in her pigtails and pink frock.

She went to open the door to get out, but Nicole stopped her. "It's alright, mum, you don't have to."

Arla sighed. Through the windscreen, she could see a gaggle of teenagers by the bus. The coach had its side compartment open, and luggage was getting loaded inside. Nicole was off on a school trip to Dorset. It was the end of June, and the last few days of school.

Nicole had been on school trips before, of course. This one was no different, but when Arla saw the teenage girls huddling together and giggling, she knew they would be up to mischief in the camp by the beach.

"Look after yourself, okay?"

Nicole appeared to resist the urge to roll her eyes. "I know, mum. You told me already."

"I'm not going to tell you not to drink or smoke." Arla looked down at her unpainted finger nails. "Like I said, that's up to you. But you know what that does to the body."

"All in good time, like Dad said last night. Right?" Nicole arched an eyebrow. And in that moment, she looked so much like Harry, Arla had to smile.

When Nicole was a baby, she looked just like Harry. A little, chubby, cute, brown baby with big eyes. And lots of spiky hair. So much that everyone commented how much hair the baby had. As Nicole had grown, her face was now more like Arla's. Nicole had Arla's brown eyes, and sharper nose.

"Yes, exactly. And don't give in to peer pressure. Hold your own."

"Lecture over?" Nicole grinned.

Arla swatted the teenager's arm. "I barely said anything. Sure you don't want me to help you with the bags?"

Nicole had a small backpack and a larger rucksack. “No,” she shook her head. Then she leaned over, and they hugged within the confines of the car.

Arla inhaled her daughter’s smell – the lavender of her shampoo, and the freshly washed clothes. She didn’t want to let Nicole go, and suppressed the little surge of emotion that tickled the back of her eyes.

“Bye darling. Take care. Love you.”

“Love you too.”

Nicole sprang out of the car, and grabbed her stuff from the back seat. She waved at Arla, then walked over to her friends. One of them spread her arms and they embraced. They laughed and chatted, and Arla was reminded of the same time in her life.

Traces of bitterness flowed with the memories. Her teenage years were difficult and lonely. No sister, no mother, and a barely present father. Nicole would have a very different life. Arla would make sure of it. She was eternally grateful that Harry had the same views as her.

With the customary forgetfulness of a teenager, Nicole didn’t even turn around as Arla turned the car around. She looked in the rear view, and saw Nicole watching her car. It was too late to wave, but Arla tried, and was thwarted by a big 4x4, driven fast by a mother who was clearly late. Arla grimaced and swerved.

She was on the main road when her radio chirped. She was the SIO for this week, and the respite was too good to last. She turned the black knob to the right.

"DCI Baker."

"PC Martinez speaking. Morning guv. Human remains found in the Regent's Canal, by Camden Lock. DI Botham there wants to speak to you."

Camden was not in Arla's jurisdiction, but she had gained quite a following for solving cold cases and using forensic anthropology.

"Patch him through."

DI Botham's warm voice came down the line. "Hi Arla, how are you?"

"Not bad, Terry. What have you got?"

"Looks like a skeleton, wrapped up in tarpaulin, with weights tied to the sides, to make it sink. Only the bones remain. Looks old. That's all I can say for now."

At least a decade old, if not older, Arla thought to herself. Terry cleared his throat. "Would you mind taking a look? I know you're busy, but we're scratching our heads."

Arla didn't have anything on her desk that needed immediate attention. That could change however. But this case intrigued her.

"No problem. Send me the location, I'll pop over now. If I do accept the case, will I be SIO, and I can bring my own team?"

"Yes of course."

Something in Terry Botham's voice told Arla he was glad to wash his hands off it. She wondered why. She pushed the thought to the back of her mind.

"Alright. See you soon."

CHAPTER 3

Arla pulled her car onto Prince Albert Road. Schools were still open, and she had to battle through the North London traffic. She heaved a sigh of relief as she got out of the car. Her phone chirped – it was Harry. He was on his way to the scene.

Arla picked her way past a cluster of uniformed officers. The morning air carried the ripe stench of exposed canal bed, centuries of decay rising from the waterway. She could see why the remains were discovered. The canal water had dropped dramatically, revealing about four feet of previously submerged wall. A stretch of dark material protruded from the mud near the footbridge, partially obscured by the shadow of a moored narrowboat. Two crime scene officers were setting up portable lights on the towpath.

She walked up to a uniformed sergeant, and showed her warrant card. His name badge said Parsons, and he nodded, and showed her the table where masks and shoe covers lay. Arla had her own sterile gloves, which she snapped on.

Scene of Crime had set up a white tent on the towpath. Blue and white crime scene tape stretched across the path, and two uniformed constables were speaking to a couple walking their dog. They were clearly not happy at being diverted. They trudged off, but Arla could see more inquisitive faces at either end of the crime scene. Both towpaths were cordoned off, and this section of the canal would now be closed for a few weeks. That would cause problems for the boats, who would have to find new routes.

Parsons was standing beside her. "Have we informed the Canals Trust?" Arla asked.

"Yes, guv. Canal traffic is getting redirected. The Lock will remain lowered until further notice. No rains now, so the water levels should stay low."

"Famous last words."

Parsons grinned and rubbed his ginger beard. "Just going by the weather forecast for July. Hope it doesn't rain like last year."

Nothing tarnished the British summer like the downpours, Arla knew. Her phone beeped again, and this time it was Dr Banerjee, veteran pathologist of the London Met. He was on his way. Arla was relieved. She didn't want to work with a brand new pathologist, and they were so critical to the case. She had worked with Dr Banerjee for so long they were practically like family. And Dr B's partner was Elaine Robinson, one of the country's best forensic anthropology experts.

Arla walked up to a narrow shouldered, young PC who was interviewing an older man in mud-caked wellies. The narrowboat resident who'd made the discovery, presumably.

Arla showed her warrant card. "DCI Baker."

"Hello, guv," the young man, called PC Holmes, straightened. His eyes gazed at her anxiously.

"Partial skeletal remains, ma'am, as you know. Mr. Martin Keane here spotted something suspicious while clearing debris from the exposed canal bed. Called it in at 9:15."

Arla nodded. She glanced at Mr Keane and PC Holmes. "Has anyone approached the remains?"

"No, ma'am. Mr. Keane says he only touched the material with his rubbish picker, backed off as soon as he realized what it was."

Arla turned her attention to the narrowboat owner. She took out her well-thumbed black leather notebook, and pen. Despite her senior rank, she knew there was no excuse to ignore the basics. Besides, the person who found the body was always a suspect.

"Talk me through exactly what happened, Mr. Keane."

“I thought I saw something dark and unusually shaped over there,” the older man pointed with a hand. “So I went to look.” He told Arla what happened.

Arla didn’t think Mr Keane was lying. He had lived his life, and she thought he had seen the worst of it. Retirement in a houseboat might well be his way of a peaceful existence.

“Why did you want to clean the canal?”

Mr Keane’s bushy eyebrows rose. “No specific reason. We live here, right? The canal’s like our home. If I moved in the future, I’d like the path to be clearer. That’s all it was.”

Arla was thoughtful. “In the recent days or weeks, have you seen anyone on the towpath acting strangely?”

Mr Keane ran a hand across his balding scalp. “Nothing that springs to mind. We do keep an eye, as you can imagine. For our own safety.”

A woman appeared on the houseboat behind. Arla saw her flowery cardigan, and matching trousers, and the make-up laden face, peering over Mr Keane’s shoulders expectantly. He turned, sensing her.

“Ah, this here’s Carol.”

Carol shuffled forward eagerly. From her inquisitive expression, Arla could tell she was dying to know more. She repeated her question. Carol thought, then shook her head.

“Just the usual dog walkers, pedestrians. People jog down here as well. Some take the short cut to the tube stop on the Lock. Usual traffic, really.” Her eyes narrowed. “Why? Do you suspect anyone of this?” She nodded towards the white forensic tent.

Arla suppressed her smile. This was a big event in Carol’s life. “Too early for suspects,” Arla said. “But if you think of anything, please let us know.” She turned to Mr Keane.

“The water level’s not been this low in ages, has it?”

“Not since the nineties, and I wasn’t even in the canals then. I hope you don’t find any more surprises.”

Arla sighed. “Neither do I.”

She gave the couple her card, and they promised to call if they remembered anything else.

Arla walked up to PC Holmes, who was fidgeting by the white forensic tent.

"I want detailed photographs of the entire exposed area," Arla instructed Holmes.

"Anything that could've been submerged at the same time as our remains. And get uniform to start door-to-door with the other boat residents. Someone might remember something relevant from back when the water was higher."

“Yes, guv, of course.” Holmes snapped to attention, and literally ran across the towpath to his sergeant.

The tent flap lifted, and the familiar figure of Henk Parmentier emerged. Arla was surprised the scene of crime officer had got here so early.

“Early bird gets the worm, eh?” Parmentier had a rueful smile on his face.

“How did you get here so quickly?”

“I was in central London, actually. Took the tube up here. DI Botham said I had clearance from you to start using their stuff.” He held up both hands and waved them. “Ta daa. Here I am.”

“Well, get yourself busy then. Got your wellies?”

Parmentier pointed at her flats, and then lifted his white space suit. Arla saw the wellies.

“Oh ye of little faith,” Parmentier sighed. “Are you going down there?”

Arla peeked under the bridge. The rusty posts were green with slime. The smell was strong enough to wake up the dead.

“No thanks. Get the remains up here. Dr Banerjee is on his way. I’ll have a look with him.”

Parmentier did a mock salute which made Arla grin. He began his careful descent to the canal bed, two crime scene officers following with their equipment.

Arla watched as they began the meticulous process of documenting the scene. The tarpaulin was heavily degraded, but its edges disappeared into the mud in a way that suggested deliberate wrapping rather than random debris. Arla could see the stones that were tied to the ends of the tarpaulin. She got closer for a better look.

The stones were tied with nylon ropes. The knots were not great, and she wasn't surprised they had come loose with time and water flows. The canals didn't have any currents, the locks made sure of that.

The tarpaulin was a large sheet, and the body, Arla could see now, had been placed inside, then wrapped around. This was a crude, hasty job, not the work of professionals. The real dealers would have cut the body into pieces, to begin with. Much easier to dispose of. This body was whole, and the skeleton was well preserved. If someone didn't want this person to be found ever again, they didn't do a great job.

The sun had fully risen now, but this section of canal remained stubbornly shadowed by the surrounding buildings. Parmentier and his team worked with steady precision, gradually exposing more of the remains. The tarpaulin had preserved certain areas better than others.

When the full skeleton was exposed, Parmentier and his helpers were assisted by two of the constables. They wrapped the skeleton in a body bag, and bought it up to the towpath. From there, it was carried inside the white tent.

Arla followed them inside. Parmentier lowered his mask. Sweat budded on his forehead.

"Found a silver necklace with pendant on the neck," he said. He extracted a specimen bag from his pocket. Arla held it up with a glove hand, against the halogen lights inside the tent.

It was a thick silver chain, but water had rusted the metal. The pendant bore two letters inside a heart shaped silver clutch – RM.

The victim's initials, perhaps?

Arla looked at the skeleton. She noted the flecks of cloth attached to parts of the bones, and the worn out, degraded shoes. Nothing but bits of black leather, stuck to the bones. The skeleton was small, no more than five feet five to seven inches, Arla thought. The skull size was not the same as a man's – it was smaller. So were the fingers and toes. From her rudimentary knowledge of forensic anthropology, she suspected this was a female.

She crouched by the skull, and ran a hand along the bone fissures that were present in every human skull. These were solid, and Dr B had once told her that was a guide to the age. Teenagers up to the age of fifteen didn't have solid, or fused, skull fissures, to allow the brain to grow.

This woman was an adult. Her jaw bones did not jut out, and again, were finely formed, like her hand and feet. Arla couldn't guess her age, but the race might well be Caucasian, or mixed.

There was a rustle at the tent entrance, and the short, bearlike figure of Dr Banerjee appear. He was dressed in his usual crumpled suit, and he had a black suitcase in his right hand. He took off his black framed glasses. His sharp, dark eyes swept over the scene, smiled at Parmentier, and then rested on Arla. Warmth lit up his face.

"Don't need me anymore, do you?" Dr Banerjee said, stepping inside. Arla was genuinely pleased to see him. The old man was like a father figure to her.

"Go on then," Dr Banerjee smiled, putting down his briefcase. "What have you found?"

"IC1 female, deceased many years ago," Arla said. "Skull sutures fused so she was an adult. Female due to her skeletal structure, pelvic brim diameter, and skull size. Also, small hands and feet. Unlikely to be a male, and not a child."

Dr Banerjee didn't blink. "Cause of death?"

"Hard to know. No visible fractures so far, but I haven't taken a close look."

Dr Banerjee glanced up and down the skeleton. Arla knew his canny eyes would miss nothing, but most importantly, he knew what he might be missing.

"We need an MRI scan of the bones, a skeletal survey. We also need to examine the rear of each bone, starting with the skull."

"That's why I'll never replace you," Arla grinned. She stepped over to him, and resisted the urge to give him a hug. She put her apron on, and Dr Banerjee did the same. They knelt by the skeleton, and Parmentier helped them gently turn the bones.

"Just the rear of the skull," Dr Banerjee said, stopping them. He took a look, and then shone his torch near the base of the skull.

"Shallow depression on the right. And a very narrow crack, likely a stress fracture that has grown bigger with time," he said. Arla was on her knees, and bent forward to have a look.

"Yes, I see it. Blunt force trauma?"

"Yes. Either a blow to the head, or she fell and hit something pretty hard to cause a stress fracture."

"Could it be the case of death?"

"Hard to know in the absence of flesh injuries. But yes, possible."

Dr Banerjee rose with a grimace. His knees popped loudly. He grunted and moved around to the middle of the skeleton. Arla let him work.

She went outside, and saw the tall, wide shouldered, lanky figure of Harry Mehta, speaking to the uniformed sergeant, on the other side of the towpath. She was Mrs Mehta, of course, officially. But at work, like many professional women, she had kept her maiden name. She would be DCI Baker until she retired. Harry, she knew, didn't mind.

He sensed her, and his head turned. Then he walked over.

CHAPTER 4

Harry stood on the bridge and tried to look down, but his height meant he had to bend very low. He stood, touching his back.

"Bad back?" Arla said. "Happens when you get old."

"Excuse me?" Harry frowned. "I'm only three years older than you."

"That's why I don't have back pain," Arla grinned. Harry rolled his eyes. They walked down to the tow path, and the mood turned sombre as Harry crouched to look under the bridge. Arla noticed Martin Keane and Carol Bainham sat on their deckchairs on Mr Keane's houseboat, watching them.

"That's where the tarp got stuck?" Harry pointed at the area under the bridge that was now circled with crime scene tape.

"Yes. It's been there a while. Years maybe. The water level going down revealed it."

"Proper job?"

"Nope. Bunch of amateurs if you ask me. Rolled the body in the tarp, tied stones to the sides and chucked it in the canal."

"CCTV?"

Harry stood slowly, and his practiced eyes looked up and down the lights of the towpath. "There," his long arm pointed to the right, across the bridge. "At least one camera that I can see. But we don't know when this happened."

"Yes. Most CCTV's were put in place in the early 2000's. Depends when this crime took place."

Harry's chestnut brown eyes focused on her. "You said amateurs. Did they leave a murder weapon?"

"No, but they forgot to take a necklace off her. I think they checked her pockets though, we can't find any other ID."

"Anything from Missing Persons Database?"

"Are you giving me orders now? I'm the SIO, remember?"

Harry shifted closer, and she averted her face when she saw the glint in his eyes. His voice lowered to a whisper. "You might be, but you were quite happy under me last night."

Arla snapped her jaws tight and stalked away. If she could reach his face she'd love to slap him. Knowing Harry, he might enjoy that too much.

Parmentier emerged from the tent, and came over when he saw Harry. One of the forensic officers was lowering a camera with a light attached, at the end of a stick. A so-called water camera, to see beneath the murky canal waters. That, Arla knew, would provide valuable information about the rest of the remains, or any other ID from the body. The divers would come later, and do a more thorough search.

Arla waved at the uniformed sergeant Parsons, who came over, with PC Holmes, and two more uniformed constables. Parmentier stood next to her, with Harry.

"Right," Arla addressed her team. "I want the scene documented and cleared before we lose the light this evening. Sergeant Parsons, coordinate with diving support – as soon as the remains are recovered, I want a detailed search of the surrounding bed. PC Holmes, get me everything you can on the bridge repairs from the past three decades – materials used, contractors, dates of work."

Parsons said, "The Canal Trust said they would send that information over. I will forward it to you ASAP."

"Good. I also want to know when those CCTV cameras were placed, and regardless of when the crime was committed, I want images analysed over the last four weeks. If this was the work of a serial killer, for instance, they often come back to their scene of crime to check their victims. Lets make sure we don't miss any weird people looking under the bridge."

The uniformed staff all nodded. Arla turned to Parmentier. "I want metallurgical analysis of the chain and pendant please." She glanced at Harry. "I've informed my team to look at Missing Persons over the last twenty years, in this region. If we hear anything, we will update you."

Arla paused. Her gaze was fixed on Parsons now. "This will be a joint South and North Command operation. My team from the Lambeth HQ will liaise with Camden HQ. I trust there won't be any problems."

Parsons cleared his throat, aware he was being put on the spot. "No. Our guv, DI Botham spoke to us about it already. We will give full cooperation to your team."

They dispersed, and Harry gave her the phone. It was Lisa Moran, her erstwhile detective sergeant in Clapham.

"Hello guv," Lisa's cheery voice came through. "Got your message and looked into missing persons. A twenty five year old woman called Rachel Matthews was reported missing, in Angel, in October 1998. That's not far from Regent's Canal according to the map."

A clutch of excitement gripped Arla's spine. "Yes, that's right. And the victim has a necklace with the initials RM. Chances are this is her."

"I'm digging into her records. She should have dental and DNA samples. Her mother reported her missing after she didn't call for three weeks. So did one of her friends. Do you want me to ring up the friend and see who else knew her?"

"No, lets wait till we get DNA confirmation. Good work, Lisa. We might have a positive ID. Start preparing a time line from the date of her disappearance."

"On it, guv."

Arla told Harry the news. He nodded. "With any luck, we could get the dental records later today."

"And we can inform her poor parents." Arla shook her head. Her heart was heavy. She couldn't imagine the trauma of not knowing, the deep anguish that had tormented the family all these years. She hoped that she could at least give them some closure.

They went inside the tent, which was a tighter squeeze now with all of them in it. Dr Banerjee listened with close attention.

"I'll prioritise this," he said. "Give me a couple of hours after I get back." He pointed at the skeleton.

"I didn't find any other injuries. No trauma to the bones, but if there was on the flesh, we'll never know. It seems the cause of death could well be that contusion in the rear occiput of the scalp. Enough force to cause a cerebral bleed, I think."

"But not enough to split her skull bone apart," Arla said. "Do you think she fell?"

"Or she was hit. Either of the two."

He pointed at the feet. "The leather from the shoe fragments might give us some clues. Not all shoes are made of the same leather." He indicated the pelvic bones.

"With a pair of tweezers I got some cloth fragments. Might be her underwear. Once the MRI scan is done we might find more cloth or other fragments on the bones."

"Thanks, doc."

Dr Banerjee smiled, and went back to his work. Arla went outside with Harry. He looked at Martin and Carol, still sitting out.

"Did they find the body?"

"Yes."

"Any other witnesses, of any sort?"

"Not so far. Let's see what the door to door and CCTV shows."

Arla looked around her. The canal itself was a kind of witness, wasn't it? The slick of water on the canal bed looked back at her as if with a baleful, secretive eye. It had lain there since the Victorian times, and held secrets deep within its dark bosom. If it hadn't been for the drought this skeleton wouldn't have been revealed.

She paused by Mr. Keane's boat. The name painted on his narrowboat's stern caught her eye: *The Borrowed Time.*

How appropriate, she thought. Time had just run out for someone's carefully buried past. The victim, Rachel Mathews. Arla cautioned herself. She didn't know for sure if the skeleton belonged to Rachel. But something in her gut told her she had found Rachel. Still, she had to wait for the DNA confirmation. And if this was Rachel – then she had a family, loved ones, who had waited decades for closure. Not knowing was always the worst part. It hounded detectives as well, pervaded their dreams at night.

Arla's jaws flexed in determination. She would bring justice for Rachel, and her family.

CHAPTER 5

It was late afternoon by the time Arla and Harry drove back to Clapham. Harry stopped the car at Angelo's café and picked up the best croissants and coffee south west London had to offer – in Harry's opinion. He picked up enough for the team, and then drove back to the nick.

Detective Sergeants Lisa Moran and Robert Pickering were at their desks and they waved at Arla and Harry. DS Ros May was also at her desk, a few metres away. She was engrossed on her laptop and didn't see them. Rob got her attention, and she walked over.

Rob rubbed his hands together, his eyes gleaming as Harry put the bag of croissants on his table.

"Thanks, guv."

"Have a quick bite, then join me in my room," Arla said. She nodded at Harry, who went to his desk, and sat down.

Arla went to her room at the rear of the open plan detective's office. It was a small space, enough for a desk and four chairs. Although Arla's jurisdiction ran to four police stations in south west London, she didn't get the plush offices her boss, Wayne Johnson had, on the top floor.

At least the sun was out. Arla stepped on the creaking floorboards, covered by the fading green, thin carpet that had lain there before she started at the Clapham Station, twelve years ago now. She flung open the curtains, and warm sunlight cascaded in, the beams blinding her.

One of the photos on her table lay on its side, and she adjusted it straight. It was her father and sister, on either side of Arla. Nicole, the sister who vanished when Arla was eleven, and whose disappearance left an endless chasm in Arla's soul. No, it would never get filled.

Next to it, was the framed photo of Harry, herself, and her daughter, Nicole, posing on a beach in Greece. Nicole was brown like her father, with frizzy black hair, and making a face at the camera. It always made Arla smile, wonder at how her little baby was now getting to her shoulder height.

She opened her laptop, and saw she had an email from Dr Banerjee. He had already got the dental record confirmation, but DNA results wouldn't be back till tomorrow. It wasn't necessary. Dental records showed the victim to be Rachel Mathews, and her ID matched the missing persons database.

Arla opened up the database on her screen. She was used to this – before she found her sister, she used to check this almost daily. She clicked on the correct Rachel Mathews, and the photo appeared on her screen.

Rachel was an attractive blonde woman, and her youthful looks twisted Arla's heart with sorrow. So young…such a waste of a promising life. She read the journal of her disappearance.

Rachel was first reported missing by her mother, and one of her friends. The date of the report was 22nd October 1998.

Her mother was Sarah Mathews, and the friend was called Julia Slater. Sarah called the police after she didn't hear from her daughter for three weeks, and when she visited the flat where Rachel lived, no one opened the door. The friend, Julia, had reported her missing on the same day as Sarah. Presumably, Arla thought, Sarah had enquired with Rachel's friends first, if she had their numbers.

There was a knock on the door, and Harry entered with Lisa, Rob, and Ros. They sat down in front of her desk, while Harry remained by the closed door leaning against it with arms folded across his chest.

"So we know for certain now," Arla began, "That the victim indeed is Rachel Mathews. What have you found out about her?"

Lisa cleared her throat, and tucked a loose, red strand behind her ear. "Rachel was a twenty-five-year-old publishing assistant at a publisher called Thames

House. They published commercial genre books in romance, crime and mystery. She was last seen at work a week before she disappeared. Witness statements from the office mention she had taken time off for health reasons. Her medical records show a history of depression, and she was seeing a counsellor, and her GP had started her on antidepressants. She had been on them for two years."

"What about her neighbours? Did they not see her in that last week? And her close friends?"

"Yes. The neighbours saw her carrying food into her flat. She lived on the top floor of a converted terraced house in Angel, Islington, in North London. The neighbours report her as a quiet person who smiled, said hello, but kept her life private. No man was seen entering her flat. She was caught on CCTV going in and out of her street. Islington had CCTV those days – mainly in the high street, but Rachel lived close to Angel tube stop."

Harry interjected. "London wide CCTV started after 1993, right? With that child abduction case, Jamie Bulger."

"Yes," Lisa said. "But it wasn't really widespread till the early 2000's. So many parts of London's residential areas still didn't have CCTV coverage. Regardless, there are CCTV footages of Rachel near the tube stop, and on her street."

Rob had his portable tablet in his hands, and he spoke up. "The footage is on HOLMES, and I've got it here. They mainly show Rachel in public spaces like the tube station, and the High Street. There's a couple where she met up with two other women. One of them is identified as Julia Slater, the woman who also reported Rachel as missing the same day as her mother did. The other is Melissa Carrington, then a trainee solicitor, and now a well-known family law barrister."

Arla said, "So Rachel was good friends with Julia and Melissa?"

"Yes. They were seen together on CCTV twice, and Melissa was also interviewed. Both her friends saw her ten days ago, caught on CCTV. They had another friend, Kate Turner. All three women were interviewed, none were treated as suspects. They exchanged text messages, and spoke on the phone with Rachel – these show up on her phone's call log. The texts and calls were normal communications – about holidays, when to meet up, what to wear, and so on."

"Good work," Harry said from behind. Arla looked up at him. Harry said, "So, these three friends are still around, right? And we can catch up with them?"

"Yes." Lisa glanced at Ros, who took over. Ros tapped on the tablet screen in her hands. Her red and white polka dot nail polish looked nice, Arla thought. Ros had come up the ranks swiftly, and made it to sergeant grade last year. Arla had mentored her, and Ros had made her proud as an excellent detective.

"Melissa, the lawyer, lives in London, I think. Her office is in a barrister's chambers in central London. She must live close by. She might be married, and her residence might be under her married name. It won't be hard to catch up with her. Julia is a counsellor and therapist for the NHS in Bexley Heath, in Kent, again not that far away. Kate Turner was harder to find. Her contact details are dead, phone number doesn't work anymore. Too many people with her name, so we need more details. Again, she might have changed her last name after marriage."

Arla pursed her lips, thinking. "Yes. Melissa was easy to spot due to her career, and like most professional women she kept her maiden name. So did Julia. As for Kate, have you checked the PCN's to see if she has a police record? Do any of them, for that matter?"

Ros shook her head. "Nope, none of them do. All squeaky clean. I searched for name changes, nationality data, nothing came up."

Harry said, "And what about Rachel's parents?"

Lisa answered. "Her mother, Sarah, now lives in Rotherham, a small town in the north east, where Rachel is from originally. Her father had a stroke last year, and died. She doesn't have any siblings."

Arla caught Harry's eyes. She knew what he was feeling. Like Sarah, they too had one child. And to imagine the horrors Sarah had endured all these years, not knowing…Arla sighed. It didn't bear thinking about.

"I will go up to Rotherham to see Sarah myself. Has anyone called her yet?"

"No, guv," Rob said. "We were waiting for your instructions."

"I will call her," Arla said. She glanced at Harry, and he nodded, indicating he would accompany her.

CHAPTER 6

Arla and Harry took the tube to Kings Cross, and Harry had bought tickets on the national railway app already. The journey would be a long one, but Arla had spoken to Sarah Mathews, Rachel's mother. The woman had known instinctively what the call was about when Arla told her it was about Rachel.

"She's not alive, is she?"

Arla's heart broke softly, without a sound. Like the falling of winter leaves, Sarah's forlorn hope had withered over time, and Arla had just dealt the final blow. There was no sugar coating this, Arla knew very well. Sarah deserved the truth.

"I'm sorry, Mrs Mathews. We found human remains that have been identified as Rachel's."

In the ensuing silence, Arla heard the sound of distant sobs. Then Sarah came back on the line.

"What happened to her? Where did you find her?"

"This will be a lot easier," Arla said gently, "If I came up to see you. Then we can talk properly. Is there a time you would prefer?"

“I’m free now,” came the prompt response. “You’re down in London, are yer?” The Yorkshire lilt in her voice was unmistakable.

“Yes.”

“Come up now if you want.”

“Are you sure you want us to come over today?”

“Yes.”

Of course, Sarah would be free, Arla thought. She had waited for this moment for so long, and now despite the awful news, she needed to know. She needed closure. Arla checked her watch, and then at Harry, who was holding up his fingers and mouthing numbers. Arla nodded at him.

“How about six thirty this evening? We should be able to take a train up.”

Arla watched the fields of barley and wheat flash past the train window. The sun was dipping on the horizon, and a flock of birds beat their tired wings across the golden sky. Going home, Arla thought. She wished that instead of herself, it was Rachel going home to see Sarah. But that would never happen. At least she could give Sarah the information she had craved for the last twenty six years.

They took a cab from the train station. Sarah Mathews lived in a nice residential street of semi detached houses and bungalows. It was more than half an hour's drive from the station. A light was on in the front porch, despite the lingering summer sun.

Harry rang the bell, and they waited for a few seconds. The house was semi-detached, and the front porch was encased by wood and glass windows. The front door opened, and a silver haired woman's face appeared. She wore glasses, fitted with a cloth chain around her neck. She stepped into the porch, and Harry opened the outer door, and held out his warrant card. He introduced himself and Arla.

"Come in," Sarah Mathews said. "I didn't think it would be anyone else."

Arla shut the door behind her. They took their shoes off, then followed Sarah down the hallway, which was wider than Arla had expected. She caught sight of framed photos of a young girl, growing up in maturity to her twenties. It was Rachel. There were also photos of a family – Rachel with her parents, and elderly grandparents, when Rachel was smaller.

After going past two closed doors, and a staircase, Sarah led them to a lounge cum diner, that opened into a kitchen. Next to the kitchen, patio doors opened out into the garden.

"Have a seat," Sarah said. The sofas were worn, and the fabric across them stretched tight, fading in places. But they were still comfortable. Arla and Harry sat down, and Sarah did the same, in an armchair with a footstool. A book lay on the footstool, and a full cup of tea next to it. The tea had not been touched. Sarah couldn't rest till she had spoken to Arla.

Arla didn't waste time. "This morning, we received reports of a human skeleton in the Regent's Canal, in North London. It's not far from Islington, where Rachel lived."

Sarah was leaning forward, her fingers clasped together, knuckles bone white. There was a tremble in her tightly drawn lips.

"DNA and dental records have confirmed it was Rachel. We looked into the missing person's report you had filed. The details are a match. There's no doubt we found Rachel's remains."

"How…how did she get there?"

Arla sighed. "At this point, we don't know. Her body was enclosed in a tarpaulin sheet, and that had sunk to the bottom of the canal. There's a drought going on currently, and the falling water levels exposed the tarpaulin. That's how the skeleton was discovered."

Sarah had stopped breathing. Her eyes bulged, and her face was white as a sheet. "Who did that to her? She was killed, wasn't she?"

"We don't know that as yet. But she did have a fracture at the base of her skull. That could be due to a fall, or she might have been hit."

Sarah stared at Arla in shock, then blinked. "Who?" She uttered a single word. Then again. "Why?"

"I'm sorry. We don't know, but I promise you I will do my everything to find out."

Sarah blinked again, then a tear drop budded in her left eye, and her lips wobbled. Her face crumpled like a piece of paper.

"My poor little girl. Oh God." Her head sank down to her chest. Arla was by her side, kneeling on the carpet. She covered Sarah's hand with hers, and the woman gripped Arla's hand tightly. Her shoulders shook with sobs.

Harry rose and went to the kitchen, and returned with a glass of water and some tissues. Arla remained where she was, till she felt Sarah was getting control of herself. She knew that Sarah had to deal with this in her own way. But she also needed more information from the woman.

Arla sat back in her chair, and glanced at Harry. She knew he wanted to look in Rachel's old room, and speak to any remaining family. But first, they needed to give Sarah some time. Eventually, the elderly woman straightened, and wiped her quivering nose. She pulled her silver hair into a ponytail.

"What do you know about Sarah's last days?" Arla asked. "You notified her as missing on 22nd October 1998. When did you speak to her before that?"

"More than three weeks before that date. I can't remember the exact date, but I'd say at least three weeks. Her birthday's on 15th October. When I couldn't take it anymore, I went down to London. I didn't have her friends' numbers, but one of them also contacted the police, the same day I reported her missing."

"Julia Slater."

"Yes. The police gave me her number and I contacted her. She was worried as well. She didn't have my number so we never spoke. I had heard from Rachel about her friends, though. Julia's name was familiar. She had also told me about Melissa and Kate. I'd seen their photos, but never met them. I recognised Julia when I saw her."

Harry asked, "Before you went down to London, did you ask Rachel's friends or relatives around here to see if they had heard from her?"

"Her school friends have left Rotherham. She had one friend from Sheffield, who moved back here. Her name's Lucy Sprowles. Lucy hadn't spoken to Julia for years. I've got a brother, who lives in Stockport, near Manchester. He didn't know anything. But David told me to get down to London. I should've done it before. Don't know why I waited so long."

"I was wondering that," Harry said softly, and Arla looked at him. Harry said, "Three weeks is a long time to not hear from your daughter."

Sarah's jaws clenched once. "She had her own life, Inspector. She was a grown woman, and she wanted to…you know. Spread her wings. Life was better in the big city. We did speak every week or so, but sometimes I didn't hear from her for more than a week."

"Were you close to her?"

Sarah inspected her nails. "She was an independent girl. She always wanted to do things her own way. I'm more of a homely person. Rach took after her dad. He was into running marathons and travelling." Sarah stopped, and Arla wondered if she left something unsaid.

Harry prompted again. "So you were close?"

"Yes, Inspector," Sarah looked at Harry with dry, empty eyes. "If you want the honest answer, she was a daddy's girl. Looked like John, too." Sarah smiled sadly, and the corners of her eyes crinkled.

"But yes, we were close, although in personality, she was like John." She stopped again, and a shadow remained in her eyes.

"Was there anything else between her and John?" Arla asked. Sarah stared at her. Arla knew she had touched a raw spot.

Sarah sighed once. "John was prone to low moods. He could spend days in his room, when he wasn't out running or hiking. He was on medicine from the doctors."

"He suffered with depression," Arla said. "Like Rachel."

"Yes. Did you get that from her police record?"

"Her medical files, which were attached. Did Rachel have suicidal thoughts? Or did she ever take an overdose?"

"No," Sarah said firmly. "Her mood spells weren't as bad as John's. She was on anti depressants, but not when she went missing. When I last spoke to her, she sounded alright."

"Did she have a boyfriend? Or partner?"

"She did, yes, but again, not at the time she went missing. A couple of years ago, she was going out with a guy called Terry. They were together for about six months."

Arla looked at Harry, who nodded. "I saw that. Terry Smith. He had moved to Australia. He did a phone interview with the police and he was cleared."

Sarah looked from Harry to Arla. "John and I stayed in London for a month. Then we kept going back to help with the police. They found nothing. Rachel was last seen walking down the high street near the Angel tube stop. Have you found anything else?"

“We’ve seen footage of her with her friends, Julia and Melissa. That was about a month before she went missing. The last sighting, as you mentioned, was by Angel tube station, on 21st October. She walked down a side street which was a CCTV dark spot. Then she wasn’t seen.” Arla opened her black leather notebook, and thumbed to the right page. “That was at 19.55 on 21st October.”

Sarah nodded, and wiped her nose. “So you haven’t found anything more than what we know already?”

“No, but its early days. Her friends had exchanged text messages with her, but they didn’t speak. Is that what they told you?”

“Yes,” Sarah said. “I wonder how close she was to her friends. I mean, she must be, otherwise she wouldn’t have told me about them. When I spoke to them, they said she had been her normal self. They were busy with work and family, and hadn’t met up recently.”

Arla wondered about that. Single women normally met up regularly with their girlfriends, unless they had a partner, husband or children.

“Alright,” she said. “Can we look at Rachel’s room, please?”

CHAPTER 7

Sarah climbed the stairs slowly, and Harry brought up the rear. Arla saw more photos of family and friends on the wall. There was a picture of a young woman sitting on a camel in a desert. Arla stopped on the landing to have a better look. It was Rachel, and she looked similar to her missing persons file photo.

"That was taken in 1996," Sarah said. "She went to Rajasthan in India, with Julia and another friend. One of the other two."

"Melissa and Kate?"

"Yes, Kate, I think. You'll have to ask them."

In the photo, there was also a white man, young, and in shorts, holding the camel's rope, and patting its neck. He smiled at the camera, like Rachel. He wasn't wearing sun glasses, like Rachel was.

"Who's the man?" Arla asked.

"I don't know. One of their travelling group, Rachel said."

They carried on upstairs, which had a bathroom, and three bedrooms. Sarah headed for the last room at the rear of the house, and opened the door. The rest of the house was dusty, and Harry had seen plates in the kitchen sink, stains on the carpet. But this room felt like it had been preserved the same way for decades. The carpet was thin but spotless, the bedsheets starched and without a crease, the books on the shelves free of dust. Sarah went to the window and pulled the curtains apart.

On the shelf, Arla saw small framed photos of a little girl with her parents. Arla and Harry put on gloves, and Arla took a closer look. She could see the resemblance between Rachel and her dad. She put the photos away. The room was an average sized double bedroom, although the single bed made it look larger.

"Mind if we have a look around?" Harry asked.

"Of course not. I'd rather stay, if that's ok."

Harry looked at Arla, and they both knew it was slightly odd, as if Sarah didn't trust them. But they agreed. Harry opened the desk drawers. He saw some old postcards, from ski resorts and beach holidays. There was some cheap jewellery in a small box with a make up mirror, and some hair ties.

Arla opened the single wardrobe, and looked through the clothes. Apart from the usual collection of old dresses, skirts, some plain underwear in a drawer, she didn't find much else. She was about to close the door, when something caught her eye. It was a black scarf, and it had fallen to the floor, next to the shoes.

It was small, not like the longer, warmer scarves women liked.

She knelt, and picked it up. It was dusty, and she covered her mouth to sneeze.

“Bless you,” Sarah said.

“Thank you.” Arla raised the scarf to the light. It was a man’s scarf; she was sure of it. The wool was thick and hairy, but it was nice and soft. At the bottom, she saw a circular design – a group of spheres of different shapes merging with each other. It was a distinctive design and not one she had seen before. She beckoned Harry over, who had a look. He grimaced.

“No idea where it’s from. Not any designer logo that I’ve seen.”

“Ok. This is too short to be a woman’s scarf, don’t you think?”

“Yes,” Harry said.

Arla showed it to Sarah, who was hovering inquisitively. “Have you seen this before?”

Sarah reached for the scarf, but Arla moved it out of her grasp. “If you don’t mind, please don’t touch. We might need this as evidence.”

Sarah looked a little annoyed, but then nodded. “I’ve not seen this before. I left everything inside as it was. Never touched anything.”

Arla thought for a minute. "When was Rachel last here?"

"April 1998. She stayed for 1 week during easter."

"I know this was a long time ago, but did she leave her clothes all packed as they are now?"

"Pretty much, yes." Sadness gripped Sarah's face. "I remember it so well. She came with her little red suitcase. These clothes you see here are her old stuff. She didn't wear them anymore."

Arla nodded, and turned back to the wardrobe. She knelt by the shoeboxes, and pulled them out. Inside, she only found old trainers and a couple of heeled shoes. She went through the clothes again, and tapped the back of the wardrobe. It was made of cheap plywood, not the type of sturdy wood that might hide a secret compartment.

Harry asked Sarah, "Did Rachel leave a phone, or laptop here?"

"No. She used to carry her laptop in a rucksack."

Harry had collected something in an evidence bag. He held it up for Arla to see. "I found this inside a box in the bottom drawer."

It was a pair of black cuff links. Arla took one out, and asked Harry to shine his phone light on it. She examined the link carefully to make sure she didn't miss an initial, or logo. She didn't find any. But something told her the scarf, and these cuff links, were a set.

"Look for men's clothes. Could be a tie, or underwear, anything," she told Harry. Sarah gaped at Arla.

"I've not seen owt like that in Rachel's room before," she said, a little impatiently.

"But we have found these now, so it makes sense," Arla said. "Did you move anything from this room?"

Sarah held her eyes. She didn't blink. "No, Inspector." Her voice was firm, and Arla nodded. She didn't think Sarah was lying. If she had moved stuff, then she would've moved the scarf and cuff links as well.

"And to the best of your knowledge, Rachel never came back here with a bloke? One that you might have missed – you might not have been present at the time?"

Sarah shook her head. "No. I would've known."

Arla pressed her lips together. "Do you mind if we have a look around the rest of the rooms? You can refuse, if you want."

Sarah's lips tugged faintly. "To be honest, Inspector, I've been waiting for some news for so long, I don't really care what you do. I've got nothing to hide. As long as you don't destroy anything, I don't mind."

"Thank you very much," Arla smiled. She could see the sadness brimming in the poor woman's eyes. "Please show us your room, and if you have any of your husband's clothes, I would also want to have a look, if you don't mind."

Sarah frowned. "Why?"

"No reason. Is that okay?"

Sarah eyed her for a few seconds, then nodded. Her posture was a little stiffer now. Harry nodded at Arla. He knew that she wanted to check if the scarf and cuff links were a match with what Rachel's father used to have.

Sarah took them to the master bedroom, and pointed at a suitcase under the bed. "John's stuff's in there. You can have a look if you want."

They did so, on their hands and knees. Harry picked out shirt and trousers, all neatly folded. He uncovered gloves, two hats, and scarves. Arla found a small box of cuff links, and a small gold ring. Arla didn't see anything that reminded her of the cuff links and scarf in Rachel's room.

They took some samples in evidence bags – Rachel's underwear, an old toothbrush. At the door, Sarah gripped Arla's hand tightly. Her cheeks were drawn and pale, the tip of her nostril red and quivering.

"Find out what happened to my girl. I need to know."

Her dark eyes held Arla captive. She felt the resolve settle deep inside her. "I will," she promised. She promised because she knew exactly what Sarah felt like. She too, had felt like that for sixteen years after Nicole disappeared.

CHAPTER 8

26 Years Ago

Rachel's heart beat faster as she stared at the tall front doors of the magnificent house. It was a detached building in Chelsea, with ivy growing on the windowsills. It was made of red brick, with white sash windows typical of a Georgian house.

"Come inside," Chris said, his hand gentle in the small of her back. He gave her a gentle, but firm, push. She stepped on the gravel, navigating her way carefully. She cursed herself for putting on heels. But she wanted to have the look today. Stylish, classy, like she knew Chris would want her to be. Sometimes, she still felt like pinching herself. What did Chris see in her? He could have any woman he wanted. With his looks and money, surely a supermodel or high-flying actress would be on his arm, not Rachel.

When she thought of the women he could be with, she felt dowdy by comparison. She had seen them, in the glitzy private clubs of Mayfair and Kensington. They came up to him like a swarm of locusts. Who wouldn't want a man that tall, handsome, and willing to splash his cash around? Rachel spotted the women in their skimpy clothes, gaping at Chris as he helped her out of his Ferrari. A bloody Ferrari! It was red as well, and Chris let her drive it once. She felt like she was flying a plane, not a car. The seats were so low she was sure her bum was grazing the road. Crazy car, and a crazy, gorgeous man.

Oh, she could see the daggers in the women's eyes when they smiled at her. She knew what the bitches were thinking. How did a plain Jane like her get to be with Chris? Well, she didn't know the answer herself. Deep inside, Rachel had her own insecurities. She wasn't the confident, outgoing type that she portrayed herself to be. But that was for another time. Tonight, she had to live up to her own, and Chris's expectations.

It was meet the parents night. Or she thought so, anyway. Chris had been his usual cryptic self, and asked her if she would like to come to his house. When she asked if his parents would be there, he smiled and said maybe.

Typical Chris. Always a man of mystery.

She held onto his elbow now for support as she stumbled over the gravel drive. She was relieved to reach the wide porch. It was made of white and grey marble, and still slippery. She pulled on his arm.

"Are your parents in?"

His blue eyes gazed at her with a hint of a smile, and his lips twitched. “Maybe, maybe not.”

He was enjoying this, she could tell. His square jaw line softened, and his cheeks dimpled when he smiled.

“You’ll be fine, don’t worry.”

Then his smile faded, and his eyes darkened. Rachel shivered. She loved that dark look in his eyes, it captivated her.

“Lets go inside.” Chris took out a set of keys from his trouser pocket and opened the door. It was dark inside, and Rachel hesitated. Then the lights came on, and she wondered if they were motion sensors, as Chris didn’t turn any switches on. She wondered why the rest of the house was in darkness.

She stepped inside a spacious lobby, which had a marble floor, like the porch. A flight of stairs went up from the left, wide enough to fit an elephant. A massive chandelier hung from the ceiling, its brilliance almost blinding her. Framed oil paintings of men and couples – two of them – hung from the walls. She imagined they would be Chris’s ancestors, or parents.

He didn’t bother to explain. Instead, he grabbed her hand, and pulled gently. There was no smile on his face. He was serious, and she shivered again. She trusted him completely, but she sensed something else in him tonight. An edge of darkness that she couldn't fathom.

"Where are we going?" She whispered. No other light came on, and they walked through a wide, but almost dark corridor.

"You'll see."

Rachel's heels clicked on the marble floor. They reached a staircase. There was a dim glow now, and it came from lights embedded in the floor. Chris gripped her hand firmly as they went down the stairs. It was a long descent into the basement. They reached a steel door that looked like a bank vault door. Chris pressed on the keypad to one side, and the door swung open.

They entered a narrower passage with a lower roof. Rachel didn't like it. She felt claustrophobic suddenly. She stopped and Chris looked at her. His face was in shadows, and she couldn't see his eyes. She felt scared.

"I don't like this place. Where are you taking me?"

"It will be nice, I promise." The smile returned to his lips, before vanishing again.

Rachel's heart was beating faster. She was torn between going forward and stopping. She looked behind once. The steel door looked smaller now, and they had advanced a long way down a tunnel, it seemed.

"Chris, what is this place?"

"It's a secret I only show to very special people," he said. He didn't even look at her, but kept staring ahead. His hand was now an iron grip on Rachel's hand. He didn't care her palms were sweaty.

He stopped before another steel door, and he looked in through the small square glass box. Then he opened the door. The lights came on inside.

"Come in." He held the door open for her. Rachel looked at him, and he smiled. "Don't be scared. It's all okay."

She stepped inside. It was a long room, with glass display cabinets stretching across both walls. Inside, she saw posters of men she didn't recognise. But they had small captions underneath, and she had to get closer to read them. But her eyes were drawn to the bed in the middle of the room, the lights around it, and the video camera on the tripod at the foot of the bed.

She also saw instruments in the display cabinets. A whip, and a selection of small knives. There was no rubber bondage outfit, but she saw hooks and nails, and photos of a woman with hooks on her back, hanging from ceiling. There were other photos of women being tortured – one woman was hog tied, and a man with a mask was piercing her back with a knife, like he was branding cattle.

Her skin crawled, and fear suddenly hit her like a tsunami. She turned around, and found Chris blocking her way.

“I want to go home,” she gasped.

“No,” he smiled easily. His eyes were dead cold. “Our fun is just beginning.”

CHAPTER 9

Julia Slater thought she could close her eyes and scream. Instead, she had to maintain a calm, professional façade, like she was listening to the weather forecast. Her client spoke in a soft voice.

"After that, I couldn't go anywhere near a man again. I mean, what happened with my uncle left me with me this…this…" He stopped and his eyes bulged, and his breathing became rapid.

"Like we said," Julia intervened. "Just stop and take a deep breath counting to four, then release counting to six. Do that twice. That's it. Once again."

After the break, the man resumed. He was speaking of the abuse he suffered at the hand of his maternal uncle, who used to sneak into his room at night. Julia had coaxed the terrible secrets out of him, like the good therapist she was. But his words were now haunting her, bombarding against the corridors of her mind. Doors she had kept shut for years were rattling, the old ghosts reaching out with their nails.

"But I'm better now," the man said. "I've joined a few dating apps. I'm still scared, but at least I joined, right?"

"Exactly. You've found out the cause of your sexual dysfunction. You know none of it was your fault and it isn't now. And you have the tools in place now to deal with the negative feelings when they arise. Correct?"

"Yes."

Julia smiled at him, but she felt a different storm raging inside her. She knew how to deal with this. It wasn't her first rodeo. Every therapist had to undergo therapy themselves to be able to shield their own psyche from triggers. She was used to it. But for some reason, today felt different. Her heart beat louder, as if whispering against her ears. A thin sheen of sweat formed on her forehead, and she breathed a little faster. She told herself there was no need to feel anxious, it was probably her hormones. She was close to her time of the month, and lately, they had been erratic.

Julia was relieved when she finished her session. She had drawn up a list of resources for her client, and he was grateful.

"You changed my life," the man said. He was of medium height, about the same as Julia's five feet eight. Emotion suffused his cheeks with patches of crimson. "When I first came to you, I was crippled with anxiety. I couldn't function. But talking to you…" the man stopped, overcome and unable to speak. Tears glistened in his eyes.

“I’m glad we could work together. You did most of this yourself. I was just the helper.”

The man raised a hand. “Oh no. You were more than a helper, believe me. I’ll never be able to thank you enough.”

Julia saw the man out, then went back to her office. She sprawled on the chair, and closed her eyes. What was the matter with her today? She needed to get back in control. She rubbed her cheeks and yawned. Her phone pinged. It was a reminder for her Pilates class this evening. She had one hour to finish her paperwork, then leave.

Her desk phone rang. She stared at it, irritated. This was a work line, and the only people who called it were the receptionists at the front desk. Julia didn’t have any clients left today, thankfully. So what were they calling for?

She answered. “Hi.”

“Sorry to bother you, Julia,” Clare, the receptionist said. “But a woman’s called for you. She’s saying it’s urgent. Her name’s Sarah Mathews. Apparently, you knew her daughter, Rachel?”

The world suddenly stopped moving. Breath got stuck in Julia’s chest like it was frozen. Her eyes dilated, and her mind zoomed back at the speed of light, so fast she felt dizzy. Words, faces, screams, tears, jostled together in her soul, then became a pin point of silent light, so bright it sizzled her eyes. She couldn't see anything.

"Julia? Are you there?"

She came back up, like a swimmer surfacing for air. "Yes. Yes, I am. Put her through. Actually no, hang on. Can you please take her number, and tell her I'll call back."

Julia wanted this call to be private. She got up and locked her door. Clare called back with the number, and she wrote it down. Then she stared at the black digits on the white paper. She didn't recognise the number or the area code. How long had it been since she spoke to Rachel's mother? A lifetime.

Rachel's mother. Why was she even calling? And why was this urgent?

A new tremor gathered in the base of her spine, and slowly made its way up to her skull. Well, there was only one way to find out. She took a deep breath, then punched the digits in. Sarah answered on the first ring.

"Julia, is that you?"

"Yes, this is me. Who is this?"

"I'm Sarah Mathews, your friend, Rachel's mother. Do you remember me?"

“I…yes…I do. It’s been a long time.” She heard the slow boom of her heart thumping, like the distant sound of cannon fire.

“I needed to tell you something. They found our Rachel. The police did, I mean. Her body, or whats left of it, was inside a tarpaulin. She was chucked into the Regent’s Canal near Camden. Can you believe it? Some bastard did that to her.” Sarah broke down in sobs.

A loud buzzing was filling every space in Julia’s head. The cacophony grew louder, harsher, till she couldn’t hear anything else. She shook her head, and put the phone down, but didn’t disconnect. She stood, then sat down again. She looked at the phone like it had just landed from Mars.

The police found Rachel? After all these years? And she was dead…Julia was zoning out, the revelations were like the whistle drops of a bombing raid, drowning her senses.

Sarah was talking again. Julia put the phone back to her ear.

“…the drought exposed a lot of the canal, they said. A houseboat owner saw the tarpaulin. I’m coming down to London soon. Will you be around, love?”

Julia was having difficulty in speaking. “I…I need to check my diary.”

A pause. Sarah said, "I know this is a lot to take in. It was for me. Are you alright?"

"Yes, I'm fine." Julia unclenched her fists. "What did the police say about what happened?"

"They don't know as yet. They think it might have been an accident, but then why would the body be wrapped in a tarpaulin? It doesn't make any sense. I think they suspect foul play." Sarah paused again. "Do you know anyone who could've done this?"

Julia swallowed the heavy weight at the back of her throat. "I don't, sorry." She was starting to get some sensation back in her hands and toes. "I can't even believe it, to be honest."

"I know. I felt the same when the police rang me. They said they would get in touch with you as well. And Rachel's other friends."

The piston beats of Julia's heart speeded up again. "Yes, that's fine. I'm not in touch with the others though, so I don't know how to contact them."

CHAPTER 10

Chris liked to visit his victims. They were his personal possessions, so to speak. He had stared them in the eye as they took their last breath. True, he had to sedate them so they would submit to his twisted desires – but what was the harm in that? He knew they enjoyed it. The hooks, needles, barbs, the bite marks he left on their skin – all of it enhanced the passion.

He could see it in their terror-stricken faces. How pure genuine terror was. There was no disguising it, was there? A human being is at her or his most transparent when they are truly terrified. When they fear what's coming next. It opens up a new dimension in their life, in their dreams – that only Chris could control. Chris had known fear like that once. He didn't like to dwell on it. He understood the contradiction. Thinking about his own terrors made him lose control. And Chris liked control. Life was like neatly arranged gift boxes. Wrapped up with a bow. Neat and clean, like the lines of tiles in his bathroom. Losing control was like smashing up the tiles.

That's why he said goodbye to his victims, eventually. Because they lost control. They couldn't face their fears, like Chris had. They didn't understand if they fought through the pain, they could be liberated. They could be free, like him. But none of them could break free of the shackles of pain. No one was brave enough to live through the torture he inflicted on them. Shame, that. He had endured the pain. His life was a mission to find a victim who could be like him.

Chris stopped on the towpath of the canal. The dull, still waters gleamed in the morning light. It was still quiet on the canal, the morning commuters didn't take this road often. That's why he liked coming here. He liked to stay by the bridge, where he knew Rachel's body was kept. It was wrapped in tarpaulin, and submerged. He enjoyed watching the still, oily water, imagining Rachel, slowly rotting away.

He thought about all his victims, but Rachel was special. She had been more vulnerable than the others. That delighted him. He loved preying on her fragilities. Make her dependent on him. Then suddenly fling the carpet from under her feet. He recalled how scared she was when she saw his torture instruments. How she cried out when his teeth sank into her flesh. For Chris, it was an invigorating memory, like the first rays of sunlight in the morning.

He quickened his pace down the towpath. He wanted to get to the bridge, stare down at the waters, watch Rachel. He smiled to himself. He needed another victim like Rachel. He had laid low for a long time now. The old urges were returning, like summer cascading back into the skies.

It was getting warm, and a woman walking her dog crossed him from the opposite side. They smiled at each other. The dog stopped to sniff at the grass on the side. The woman pointed down the towpath, which curved slightly to the right. The view ahead was hidden by a bank of trees.

"There's police up there. They've blocked the path. You can't get through. I came down a side path."

A trickle of concern slid down Chris's spine. "Oh really?" He acted calm. "Do you know why?"

"Well, the police won't say. But one of the houseboat owners was saying they found a body. The drought has lowered the water levels, and the body got exposed. Ghastly, isn't it?"

Chris forgot to breathe for a few seconds. Then his mouth opened in an expression of sympathy.

"Yes, how awful. How long has the body been there for?"

"Don't tell anyone", the woman lowered her voice. She was in her sixties, with her hair pulled back in a ponytail. She wore a purple frock and had red nail polish on. "But I heard it's a skeleton and it was inside a cover or something."

The woman looked suitably shocked, and shook her head. “Unbelievable. Who would’ve though, eh?”

Chris’s heart was beating faster, and he could feel a warmth in his neck. “Terrible. Anyway, nice meeting you. See you later.”

He smiled and walked on, aware the woman was a little put out by his sudden departure. He walked fast around the gentle curve, and then he saw it. He halted. A few uniformed police officers stood on either side of the bridge that spanned the canal. A white tent had been erected on Chris’s side, on the right. He watched as a woman emerged from the tent. She had a sharp, pinched expression on her face. Her chin and cheeks were all angles and bones, and there was a quick look in her eyes as they scanned the crime scene. She was followed by a man much taller than her. They took off their white disposable aprons. They wore suits, and Chris imagined if they were detectives.

He got closer, then stopped again, watching the houseboat owners on the decks of their boats. He knew what they were saying.

“Rachel,” Chris whispered under his breath. “They found you.” Anger jolted in his heart. This wasn’t right. Rachel was his and always would be. How dare the police get their dirty hands on her?

He went off the towpath so he wasn’t that visible. He pretended to go down the side path that veered off to the right, but instead, he trampled over the undergrowth and stayed behind the trees till he was abreast of the crime scene. He could see the white tent clearly now, and that woman detective, deep in conversation with her tall male colleague. The uniforms were guarding the area, and if he got closer, he would be spotted. And so what if he was? An idea came to him, and he grinned.

The police had corrupted Rachel's peaceful resting place. Surely he was allowed to get closer, pay his last respects?

Chris shuffled forward. One of the uniformed officers was speaking to a group of onlookers. Chris stepped over the low fence, and back into the towpath. He got closer to the crime scene, and now the detectives glanced at him. The uniformed officers started to turn in his direction.

"Boxer!" Chris called out, looking around him. "Boxer! Where are you?"

The uniformed officer came up to him. "I'm sorry, sir, but you can't be here."

"It's my dog, Officer. He just ran out from the bushes. Have you seen him? He's a cocker spaniel, golden coat."

"No, sorry. But you can't be here, sir."

"Oh," Chris looked anxiously towards the canal. "What if he fell in the water?"

The officer looked perplexed. “I didn’t see a dog…stay here, sir, and I’ll ask.” He went away and spoke to a couple of his colleagues. They shook their heads, and came back. Chris was closer now, and he heard someone call out – “DCI Baker. Call for you.”

The female detective turned and walked to a man in a crumpled suit. DCI Baker. Now Chris had a name.

The uniformed officer came back. He spread his hands. “No dog’s been seen around here, or gone into the canal. Are you sure your dog was here, sir?”

The man had a steely look in his eyes, and he was looking Chris up and down. Chris didn’t want to push it too far. He glanced once at the white forensic tent, aware Rachel was lying there. He wished he could see her one last time, but it wouldn’t be the same as his cherished memories. Well, he could hold on to those.

“Thank you, officer,” he smiled. “He must be around; I’ll take a look.”

CHAPTER 11

Arla was at work early the next morning. It was seven am when she walked into the Clapham Police Station. As usual, she walked from the Clapham common tube station, and enjoyed the summer morning walk. The leaves in the Common trees were green now, and there was the hum in the air – birdsong, squirrels in the branches, the green grass luminous in the morning rays. South London was waking up to summer, and the verdant expanses of the common were the best places to enjoy it.

At the front desk, there was the usual smattering of drunks from the night before. The duty sergeant saw her and waved. Arla waved back, and Adam pressed the button under the counter. The bullet proof double doors at the rear of the chamber slid open, and Arla stepped through. The green lino of the corridor had seen better days, but the walls had a recent lick of paint, courtesy of the tax payer. Arla nodded at the uniformed officers and detectives who walked past her. The male detective officers reserved a certain disdain for her. It came with her senior position.

Justin Beauregard, one of the Detective Inspectors, went past and barely glanced at her. He would never get over the fact that Arla had got a higher rank than him. The fact that she was a better detective, and had a much higher successful prosecution rate than him, didn't seem to matter.

Rob, Lisa, Ros and Gita hadn't arrived as yet. Harry was also at his training to become an Authorised Firearms Officer, or AFO. Arla wasn't happy about that, but Harry wanted to do it. She couldn't stop him. She also couldn't bear the thought of Harry being involved in counter terrorism operations, or chasing after armed criminals. But it's what he wanted, and she had to accept it.

She stopped at the canteen and picked up a muesli yogurt and coffee, then went to her office at the rear of the open plan area. In her room, she pulled open the curtains, then fired up her laptop. She took out her trusted black leather notebook, where she had written down a few things when she spoke to Sarah Mathews.

Arla looked up Rachel's father, John Mathews. He didn't have any PCN's. Arla had his photos, and she had already sent the image to the team. Gita had done an image identification search on HOLMES, and not found anything. Arla repeated the process now, and also checked on the CSODS or child sex offender disclosure scheme website. She didn't find any matches with John's name. Satisfied, Arla did the same with Sarah, and she got the same results – nothing.

She had received Rachel's medical records, and looked through them. Rachel had suffered with low mood and anxiety as a teenager. She had been referred to CAMHS, or the child and adolescent mental health service. She used to self harm, and had once taken an overdose. Her mental health seemed to have improved as she got older. But aged twenty-one, when she was living in in London, she was started on antidepressants by her GP in London. Arla checked the list of medications to see if she could spot an antipsychotic. She wasn't a doctor obviously, but she had dealt with a couple of cases where a paranoid schizophrenic murdered someone as they felt they were following them.

She didn't find any other medications. Rachel, she thought, suffered with depression and anxiety, but it wasn't severe, and Arla didn't think suicide would be a cause of death. Rachel held down a job, she had friends and a social life. She had done well in university, passing with a first-class honours degree. That didn't sound like a woman crippled by depression.

Her mind went back to the lack of information on Rachel's boyfriend, or partners. Her boyfriend in Rotherham had been checked out, but who was Rachel with in London. She arrived in London at the age of twenty-one and lived there till twenty-five –

and she had an active social life. She must've had a boyfriend or two.

Arla's mind went back to the scarf and cuff links she found in Rachel's wardrobe in Rotherham. She went through the photos she had taken, zooming into the design on the scarf. It was made of five concentric circles, all merging into one another – like a Venn diagram, but with multiple circles. Arla had never seen the image before.

She remained convinced the scarf and cuff links belonged to a man – but who? It wasn't John's. Rachel had taken them up north in her suitcase – for what reason? Was she pining away for a man she missed? Or was there another reason. In any case – Arla had handed over the material to the lab, and Parmentier would do a search for DNA samples.

Arla sipped her coffee and checked the crime report scene from 24th October 1998, two days after Sarah and Julia Slater had reported Rachel missing. That's when the police broke into the flat. Rachel's personal belongings were present. But there was no sign of anyone else living there – a man in particular. Arla read the witness reports of Rachel's neighbours.

She read one account with interest. An elderly neighbour on the ground floor had seen a "nice sports car, maybe a Porsche, but what do I know," drop Rachel off one night. It was late, and this elderly lady didn't sleep well at night. She had seen the car drop Rachel twice in October.

There was no CCTV on that road in 1998. Arla doubted anyone had followed up on what this woman said. It was a vital clue, but she didn't see any of the detectives following up on it. Suicide had been the general consensus, and the matter was put to rest when nobody turned up. Rachel's friends – Julia, Melissa and Kate – had all agreed that Rachel's worsening mental health was the reason for her disappearance.

But Arla wasn't so sure. At the very least – she wanted to keep an open mind.

Rachel's flat was in a good state. She didn't have signs of neglect. Plates were not stacked in the kitchen sink, the furniture was well looked after, Rachel's clothes had been ironed and folded.

Arla knew people in deep depression, those who committed suicide, were often incapable of looking after themselves. They often drank excessively or took drugs – and neither had been noted on Rachel's medical records. The condition of her flat certainly didn't show Rachel was in a long term depressed state of mind.

Arla ploughed on through the detective's report from 1998. A photo was present – of Rachel and her three friends in a frame, all four of them happy and laughing. Sadness clouded Arla's heart when she saw the young, confident faces, particularly Rachel's.

“What happened to you, Rachel?” She whispered. “Where did you go?”

CHAPTER 12

There was a knock on the door and Gita Chaudry came in. Her black hair was tied up in a ponytail and she wore a lilac cardigan over cream-coloured slacks.

"Hi guv. Sorry I missed you yesterday. Can I come in?"

"Yes of course," Arla smiled and waved her in. "How are you?"

"Not bad, guv. Good to be back." Gita had taken a short leave after her break up from a twelve year long relationship. The apartment she shared with her partner had to be sold, and Gita now rented a smaller apartment. She came in, clutching a tablet device in her arms, and a folder of papers.

Arla noticed she had lost weight, and she seemed to be weighed down under an invisible cloud. Gita smiled, but it didn't quite touch her eyes.

"You're early," Arla said. "Have the others not arrived yet?"

"Ros should be here soon. She sent me a text she's on her way. Not sure about Lisa and Rob." Gita sat down.

"Ros and I looked into the flat where Rachel Mathews lived, and the neighbours' statements. Back in 1998, the CCTV was patchy in that part of Islington, unfortunately. So we found some CCTV footage of Rachel, but Rob told you about them, didn't he?"

"Yes. And I've just read the old lady's report, who saw Rachel getting dropped off by a sports car, maybe a Porsche, late at night. She saw it twice."

"That's correct. No other neighbour had seen it. The couple who lived in the flat opposite Rachel also wrote that three of her friends came to see her a few times. The woman in the flat, a Mrs G, saw them in the landing. They were dressed to go out." Gita opened her up tablet and flicked to the witness statement. "Two of those three friends turned out to be Julia and Melissa. But we don't know the third woman."

Arla was checking her own notes. "It wasn't Kate Turner? That was the third friend, according to Julia and Melissa."

"No, because Kate Turner denied having been to Rachel's flat."

"Really? So who did the girls say she was? I mean, Julia and Melissa must know if they were present that night?"

"They were vague on the subject. Both of them. A friend of Rachel's, from work, they said. Julia and Melissa didn't know her name."

"And what did her work place witnesses say? If a work colleague was close enough to visit her at home, the police should've spoken to her, correct?"

Gita checked her screen again. "They did speak to her work colleagues. I've got some names here. But none of them had been to her flat."

"So, we don't know the identity of this third woman who came to her flat, and who was seen by the neighbour on more than one occasion?"

"Correct. It seems the police didn't identify her either. She clearly wasn't a work colleague. Or maybe she was, but then left Thames House, the publishing company Rachel worked for."

"We need to find that woman." Arla sighed, and pressed her lips together. "How could the detectives back then not chase this?"

"I don't know, guv. They also didn't find a boyfriend. I mean, Rachel lived an active social life, it seems. How could she not have a boyfriend?"

"My sentiments precisely," Arla said. "Especially if the elderly lady saw a car drop Rachel off late at night. How could they not have picked that car up on CCTV?" Arla raised a hand. "I mean, Rachel's street might not have CCTV, but would they not have seen it on the main road?"

Gita downturned her lips, and her shoulders rose. "I don't know, guv. There was nothing in the reports."

Arla frowned. "Why? Did the SIO at the time justify that?" Arla knew the senior investigating officer would have the final say in what line of investigation was followed. A Porsche that dropped Rachel off late at night in front of her flat was a big red flag. Even in 1998, despite the lack of universal CCTV coverage in London, Arla would've moved heaven and earth to find the owner of that car.

That bothered her, sitting at the corner of her mind like a little rat nibbling away. "What was the SIO's name again?"

Gita consulted her file. "DI Brian Dempsey. He retired in 2006."

"Eight years after Rachel's case. He must've been in his late sixties then. Let's say sixty seven, shall we? Two years after the state retirement age. That puts him at fifty eight years old in 1998."

"Fifty-nine," Gita corrected.

"Maths was never my strong subject," Arla grinned. "Okay, so late fifties." Her smile faded. "He would be an experienced DI, in my opinion. He worked in the Islington office of the London Met, right? North West Division."

"Yes, correct."

"So there's a woman who came to Rachel's flat more than once, and a car that dropped her off. That car could well be driven by a man. I'm making assumptions here – but let's face it, there's more chances a man drove that nice Porsche."

"I think so too, guv. Do you want me to track down Brian Dempsey? See where he is now?"

Arla lowered her head. Then she nodded. "He will be in his eighties. Might not be alive anymore. Let's check that he's around. Okay?"

"Alright, guv."

There was a knock on the door, and Lisa and Ros came in. Ros carried a tray with five steaming cups of coffee.

"Woman after my own heart," Arla said, standing to make room for the tray on her desk. She had a lot of papers on her in-tray that she needed to sort out. As the Inspector responsible for five police stations in south west London, Arla's admin responsibilities were high. She didn't like that part of her job, and it involved toeing the line of the Assistant Commissioners of the London Metropolitan Police Force – the top brass.

But her heart now lay with discovering what happened to Rachel. She couldn't rest till she had more answers.

"Right," Arla said, taking a sip of her second cup of coffee that morning. "Let's set up a timeline for Rachel, shall we?"

Arla went to the white board in the corner of her office, and raised the paper to a clean sheet. She wrote Rachel's name at the top, and wrote number one.

"Rachel was last seen two nights before she was finally reported missing. So, on 20th October, 1998. When she left her flat, and she's picked up on CCTV walking to the tube stop. She gets on the tube and then we lose her."

Arla took a sip of her coffee, then continued. "For almost three weeks, she wasn't in touch with her mother. We never found her phone, so we don't know if she stayed in touch with friends, but her friends say that she did. And there was nothing unusual about her texts and calls."

"That's from Julia, Melissa and the as yet elusive Miss Kate Turner." Lisa said. "We still haven't spoken to them."

"But we have set up times to meet them," Ros said, turning to Gita, who nodded. "Julia Slater is booked in for half eleven this morning, at her clinic in Cadogan Square, in London."

"Very posh," Arla said. "That's like London's jewel in the crown. I thought Julia worked at a National Health Service Clinic in Bexleyheath?"

"Yes, she does, but the Cadogan Square is her private clinic. She did sound posh on the phone, I must say." Gita and Ros exchanged a glance.

"Okay, and what about Melissa and Kate?"

"Melissa will be this afternoon at two PM. Neither Julia nor Melissa have access to Kate Turner any more. I don't know why. They say she changed her number, got married, and moved away."

Ros said, "But we checked her witness statement. She had to put her home address there, and from the electoral roll and council tax records, we managed to trace her. Yes, Kate did get married, but then she also got divorced. No children. She now lives in Broadstairs, in Kent."

"That's a well-known beach spot, correct?" Arla raised her eyebrows. "Think I went there once, many years ago."

A distant memory struck her. She couldn't have been any more than nine, or maybe ten. In a rare day of happy sunshine, her dad and older sister Nicole, had taken the train from London for a fun day out. Then light turned to rust as Nicole's face came to her mind, then vanished in a wave of despair. The little moments caught her unawares, and the pain was almost visceral. Arla blinked, trying to get back to the present moment.

"That's right," Lisa said. "Darwin's Bay is one of the best beaches in Kent. That's in Broadstairs." She glanced at Ros and Gita. "Have we tracked Kate Turner down there?"

"Yes, I've got her address and phone number – again from the council, but also gas and electric bills. She's not responded to calls or texts so far. So I sent her an email, but not heard back as yet."

"Hmm." Arla narrowed her eyes. "Any PCN's? Police record?"

"None that we found," Gita said. "I found her name on a magazine article. I think she works for the Kent Gazette, a lifestyle magazine. There can't be two Kate Turners in Broadstairs who are both fifty-one years old, and journalists."

"Okay. Set up a meeting with her, and make it urgent." Arla returned to the white board.

"Right, so on the 20th October, Rachel goes out, into the tube station, and then vanishes. When was she sighted before that?"

Gita said, "On CCTV, she was seen in Soho, near Charing Cross Road, the week before. That's where she worked. She was actually off that week, for annual leave. She was seen coming out of the tube station, and going into the Thames House office. The offices are on the second floor of a building in Soho."

Ros nudged her, and Gita held up the tablet device. "I've not looked at the CCTV images. Shall we check them? I got hold of it late last night."

"No time like the present."

They gathered around Arla's desk, and Gita played the footage. Rachel's figure was circled in red, and they watched the grainy black and white image as she came out of Charing Cross Road tube station, waited at the traffic lights, then crossed the road. The film followed her till she went up to her office.

"No CCTV in her office, right?" Lisa asked.

"Nope," Ros answered. "It wasn't a legal requirement in 1998, and Thames House was a small business back then."

Gita played the footage again, and they watched Rachel, again encircled in red, come out of the office. The picture quality was worse than what Arla was used to now. There was a reason of course, in 1998, CCTVs were much more basic, and these old cameras didn't have digital footage. All the old cameras had their feeds converted to digital feeds in 2006, and Arla knew she was lucky to find any films of Rachel at all.

They followed the red circle as Rachel walked past the tube stop, and kept going. The camera picked her up again in a narrow street in Covent Garden. She stopped outside a pub, and spoke to a man. Then she went inside with him.

"Zoom in," Arla said. She pointed at the screen, squinting. "Look. They're touching hands."

“And standing very close,” Gita said. “They were together, weren’t they?”

“I think we just found the missing boyfriend,” Arla said. “Or someone she was dating.”

Gita enlarged the man’s side profile. No other angle was visible. “That should be enough,” Arla said, “to use image recognition software for a match, correct?”

“We can certainly try. He’s partially turned to the camera, so it’s more than a side profile.” Gita said.

“Right, guv. Shall we watch the rest? There might be better images.”

“Yes.”

Gita pressed play again, and they watched as Rachel and the man emerged. Only Rachel was circled in red. They walked together, and although they didn’t hold hands, they walked close. At the bottom of the street, they went separate ways.

“That’s all we have from her final week. There’s two more films, both similar. Do you want to see them now?”

Arla was inspecting the man’s image. They now had a better, frontal view of his face. He was young, similar age to Rachel. He had a light stubble on his cheeks, and was taller than Rachel, about six feet.

“Good work,” Arla said, her eyes shining with excitement. “Get the match done, ASAP.”

Gita nodded and left. Ros took over, and played the rest of the films. It showed, as Rob had mentioned earlier, Rachel and her three friends walking in Leicester Square. The usual crowds were present, but not excessive.

Arla asked Ros to zoom in and she got a good look at the faces of Julia, Melissa and Kate. Through the rest of the film, they saw the women walk around, then separate to go their own ways. Rachel walked to the Picadilly station. There, she stopped to speak to the same man they had seen earlier. Together, they went down the underground steps, and disappeared.

Arla frowned. A worrying buzz was intensifying in her ears, like the drone of a crazed, nuclear-powered bee.

"We need to find this man. Why was he not flagged up before?"

CHAPTER 13

Melissa Carrington took off her barrister's wig and sighed. She was in the King's Counsel Common Room now, the haloed halls of Grey's Inn, one of London, and the world's, premier legal institutions. The case she had dealt with had been difficult. A violent argument between a divorcing couple had turned to tragedy. They were still living in the same house, and both were wealthy, but the sprawling mansion was the man's main asset, hence he refused to move out. He had fallen down the stairs – slipped, his wife said. Pushed – the man's adult children said, but they were not present. The children, and family, maintained the wife married the older man for money. The wife denied it obviously, and Melissa was the woman's counsel.

It was a high value case, with assets totalling twenty-five million pounds. Melissa only took high value cases. She was now a King's Counsel, or KC barrister. She had *taken silk*, in legal parlance, which referred to the silk cravat the Victorian barristers used to wear. KC barristers could charge in excess of one thousand pounds per hour, and only the richest people could afford them.

“Tough recital?” a voice said behind her. She turned to see Michael Frimley, another barrister, with a cup of tea in his hand.

“You could say that,” Melissa said. “I think we’ll win, though.”

“Sure you will,” Michael grinned. “See you later.”

Melissa watched him vanish through the tall, oak panelled doors of the centuries old Common Room. She took out her phone and checked her messages. Her younger teenage boy had sent a photo of him and his girlfriend in Dorset. He was Finn, the sixteen year old. Melissa sent back a smiley face and heart emoji.

She got a news alert, and clicked on the link. A body had been discovered in Regent’s Canal, near Islington. No other news had been revealed. Melissa knew how the police worked – they had been forced to make a press release – but they revealed the least information.

Melissa was going to dismiss the report. Many people had died in the canal, she was sure. The faint tremor of memory in the depths of her soul was a little spark of anxiety. She squashed it with her usual brusqueness. She had no time to deal with random crap.

But something made her read the rest of the report. The nosey reporters had spoken to the houseboat owners who lived on the canal. The body was wrapped in tarpaulin and it might be a skeleton –

unconfirmed report from sources. Typical journalist speak which meant they were digging for dirt.

But the location bothered Melissa. She looked at the photo. The woods on either side, the towpath…. suddenly her chest constricted, and her eyes dilated. Her mouth opened to breathe faster. She read the beginning of the report again. It was in Regent's Canal.

Melissa put the phone down. She walked to the window, and stared out at the green park below. London's skyline formed concrete questions marks on the horizon. The past screamed back at her with a banshee wail, then vanished. Visions rained on her mind like shards of exploding glass. She turned away, and checked her phone, on reflex. There was no other news.

It was a coincidence. Many people died by the canals, over the years. But her sense of disquiet remained. She got changed, and went downstairs. She entered her office, and spoke to her clerk. She had some phone calls to return. Melissa got busy with her work. Around ten in the morning, the phone on her desk rang. It was her clerk.

"A detective constable from the London Met wants to speak to you. She said it's confidential."

Melissa knew then. That little spark of anxiety was slowly kindling into a flame. But it was okay. The past was the past – nothing could be changed. The stories remained the same. But she didn't like the tremor that ran down her spine, spreading to her fingertips. She clutched the receiver tightly.

"Put her through."

"Melissa Carrington? This is DS Ros May speaking."

"Hello. How can I help?"

"We would like to speak to you in person about a cold case. It concerns a missing person called Rachel Mathews. She was your friend, and you gave a statement regarding her disappearance."

Melissa paused. "Gosh. That takes me years back. Yes, of course. What's going on?"

"Human remains were discovered in Regent's Canal near Islington. DNA and dental checks have revealed the remains belonged to Rachel Mathews."

There it was. The words were like a sledge hammer to her heart. She felt vacant inside, like air was sucked out of her lungs.

"Oh God. You found Rachel?"

"Yes, Miss Carrington."

Melissa felt a black weight lodge in her throat, and emotion rose into her eyes. She sniffed and she wiped away the moisture. She sighed, and gathered herself.

"I'm sorry. It's just a..."

"Don't worry. Would it be possible to see you later this morning? Or maybe this afternoon."

Melissa checked her diary, a task she would normally assign to her clerk. She arranged to see the detective at half past two. That gave her about five hours to get on with her day. She hoped she could have a clear head when she saw the detectives.

She wondered about Julia and Kate. Names that now sounded like strangers to her, but the bonds that tied them once had been strong.

CHAPTER 14

26 years ago

Rachel held her head in her hands. Her breath came in gasps, and her body shook with pain. Chris had overpowered her, forced her on the bed. He had tied her hands and then….she shuddered. She had submitted eventually, and endured the onslaught. She never wanted to see him again. But once he saw her distress, he had untied her, and apologised profusely.

"I'm so sorry," he said, kneeling in front of her. "I thought you were enjoying it. I didn't realise…"

"Just take me home," she had whimpered. For once, he had listened. It was late when he dropped her off home. That night, Rachel found sleep difficult. He had hurt her, and she couldn't sit properly. Despite the late hour, she called her friend, Kate.

"I'm coming over," Kate said.

"No, it's okay. I'm exhausted and I just want to sleep."

"You can't go on like this, Rachel," Kate's voice was firm. "Enough is enough. You need to tell the police."

"I can't. You know why."

"No, I don't. Just because he's rich? How many other women do you think he's done this to? If you don't say something, I will."

"I…I don't know. I just need to rest."

Kate's voice was soft. "I'm sorry, darling. Are you sure you don't want me to come over?"

"No, it's okay."

Rachel met with Kate and Julia the next morning, in St James Park near Buckingham Palace. They found a quiet spot by a pond, under a weeping willow tree. It was winter, and the pond was half frozen. A crow sat on the frozen waste, pecking at a dead fish.

"Rachel, you need to stay away from this man. Do you understand?"

"I know that," Rachel said. She inspected her nails. "We both like that…that violent sex thing. I don't mind when there's a bit of slapping. That's what got us together. But now it's something else. And the place where he took me last night…you should've seen it." Rachel described the basement of the massive house in Chelsea.

"Sounds like a torture chamber," Kate frowned. "Rachel, you need to report this to the police. I'll come with you."

Rachel shook her head. "What will the police do? He's got glass cabinet displays, that's all. He's not breaking any laws."

"Have you spoken to Melissa about it? She's the lawyer."

"No." Rachel looked at her friend. "Do you think I should? I've talked to Julia."

Kate nodded, understanding in her eyes. There was more to this than either of them could say out loud.

"I think the three of us need to meet up soon." Kate sighed, and looked towards the frozen pond. The crow flew away, leaving the carcass of the fish it was nibbling. The sky was a vivid, cold blue.

"How long has this been going on for?" Kate asked.

Rachel didn't answer immediately. Kate said, "You're into that type of sex? I didn't know. Always the quiet ones, right?" She turned to her friend, a small smile on her lips. It faded quickly.

"That's what drew us together. Yes, the pain turns me on. But not too much, otherwise it takes over."

Kate stared at her in silence, then grimaced. "Rachel, that's weird. You know that, don't you?"

Rachel closed her eyes and her head sank down. "Oh god. Yes, I do now. It's gone too far. I don't know how to stop it."

"If you don't, then we will," Kate said, determination flashing in her eyes.

CHAPTER 15

Arla was on a long-distance phone call to Terry Smith, Rachel's last known boyfriend.

"Thank you for taking the time to speak to me," Arla said. "I know it's late in Sydney."

"Ten pm, to be precise. But no problem. I understand the urgency. Have you really discovered Rachel's body? How?"

"It was wrapped in tarpaulin and thrown in the canal with stones tied to it. London is going through a drought currently, and heat levels are high. Water levels are down. That's what exposed the tarpaulin."

Terry couldn't speak, then he swore softly under his breath. Arla said, "You and Rachel were together for six months in 1997, is that correct?"

"Around that time, yes. But we were together longer than six months. I was thinking about this since I heard the news from your detective constable. In November 1997 I went to Australia. Rachel and I were going since December 1996. She came to my parents house for Christmas. That's how I remember. We broke up next year, around October, I think."

"So you were together for almost a year. What do you remember of Rachel?"

Terry paused. "She was a wonderful person. On the quiet side, till you got to know her well. Although she was reserved with strangers, she could really be the life and soul of the party in a small group. But in a big crowd she was shy."

"What else? Did she have spells of low mood? Was she sad?"

"There was that, yes. She could be prone to mood swings. Not angry or shouting, she could slip into being very quiet. It didn't last long. I knew she had taken anti-depressants before. I don't think she took any while we were together."

"You don't think?"

Another pause. "If she did, she didn't tell me. We didn't live together. I did see her bouts of low mood, but they didn't last for long. It didn't affect her life in a bad way. It didn't spoil our relationship."

"What made you break up?"

Terry sighed. "What causes the end of any relationship? We wanted different things. I wanted to see the world, and my Aunt and her family live in Sydney. I've been here as a child. In my career as a Physiotherapist, I could do much better in Sydney.

She didn't want to leave, and I didn't blame her. Her family were in England."

"Did you meet her family??"

"Yes. Once. I went up to Rotherham. Saw her mother for a weekend. That was it."

Arla thought for a while. She didn't remember Sarah mentioning Terry visiting. It might've slipped her mind. That made her think of the man's scarf and cuff links in Rachel's wardrobe.

"Mr Smith, I know this was a long time ago, but do you recall leaving any of your clothes behind in Rotherham, when you visited? I'm talking specifically about a scarf and a pair of cuff links."

Terry was quiet for several seconds. "Like you said, many years ago, but no, I don't recall leaving anything up there. Sorry."

"No problem. Anything else you want to say about Rachel?"

Another pause. "Like I mentioned, she opened up more on a one to one. Parties were not her thing, unless it was only close friends."

Arla wondered if Terry was trying to tell her something. "When you were alone with her, in what way was she different?"

The pause was longer this time. Then Terry cleared his throat. His voice was lower. "I mean, uh, I'm not sure how to put this. And I don't want to say anything that might be taken the wrong way."

"Can you please say it? Anything you recall will help us."

He was quiet again, and Arla was getting concerned. Was she wrong not to have considered Terry as a suspect? In fact, she was beginning to doubt a lot that she had learnt about Rachel so far. Arla suspected the woman had a hidden personality no one knew about.

"Mr Smith?"

"Yes." Terry sounded like his mind had wandering far and wide, and he had to bring it back to focus. "Sorry. I…I didn't mention this before. And I don't want to get into trouble for doing so."

"You're not in any trouble."

"Alright. Rachel…she liked a bit of slap and tickle. I don't mean just some rough sex. It was more than that. She…"

Arla was getting a strange feeling. "Go on."

"She liked me to hit her. I refused of course. That's not how I get off. God, I can't even believe I'm telling you this."

"I can see why you wouldn't have, all those years ago. You didn't want the police to think you were weird, or even responsible for her vanishing."

"Oh my god. You're totally right. I guess it doesn't matter anymore, right?"

Arla knew Terry wouldn't be so open with her if he had anything to hide. She had checked his background. He was clean, but more importantly, Arla wasn't getting any weird vibes from this man. His voice was open, relaxed. Arla knew she had to keep an open mind. If Terry was a killer, it would be a nightmare to bring him to justice. But if he was – then would he really be telling her these secrets?

"Carry on," Arla urged. "Be as frank as you need to."

Terry sighed. "Oh dear. Okay. At first, she wanted me to slap her, then tie her up and throttle her. It proceeded to punching her in the belly. Look, I know how weird this sounds. To be honest, I only did that once. I'm not the kind of guy who hits women. But the one time I did that, she was in pain, but she also loved it. We had great sex afterwards – driven by her."

"Did she really want you to hurt her?" Arla's mind was spinning loops. She didn't expect this. It was completely off the scales in terms of weirdness.

"Yes, she did. But there was a line she wouldn't cross. For example, she wanted me to strangle and slap her, but not to the extent that she got seriously hurt. She was okay with the bruises. As long as they weren't on her face."

Terry was silent for a while. "Oh God. I know how this sounds now. Maybe I shouldn't have said anything."

"No, you did the right thing."

"In the end, I wasn't comfortable with it. I think she also realised it was bizarre. I asked her if she had always been this way. She wouldn't say yes or no. But in any case, – we stopped those bizarre nights. I could tell she wasn't as excited by our lovemaking anymore."

Terry exhaled, as if he had shifted a weight that had lain on him his whole life. "I'm not going to be in trouble for this, am I?"

"No. Who else knew about this? Her close friends?"

"I don't know. We didn't discuss that."

"Did you stay in touch with Rachel after you split up?"

"For a while, yes. We remained friends. I think I last sent her a text in the middle of 1998. It was winter here, so summer back in England."

"How did she sound? Was she in another relationship?"

"She sounded alright, to be honest. She had a new job, and yes, a new bloke as well. We didn't talk, only texted. I didn't hear from her after that."

"Did she by any chance send you a photo of her partner? Or tell you his name?"

"No, she didn't, and I didn't ask. We had moved on, to be honest. I was starting to feel I shouldn't be in touch with her. I was with my wife by then, although we weren't married. I did get the impression Rachel found it hard to move on. We broke up mutually, but she was the one who stayed in touch. She wanted to come over to Australia. That never happened."

Something in his voice told Arla he was glad he didn't see Rachel again.

"Thank you, Mr Smith. You have my number, and I will email you my details. If you remember anything, please contact us."

"I hope you find what happened to her. I really do."

CHAPTER 16

Kate Turner was at her desk when her boss came over. Jeff was balding, in his late fifties, with a pot belly that suggested many solitary evenings in the front of the TV with booze and snacks. But he made an effort at work, and was dressed in a nice blue suit that strained his protruding abdomen.

He leaned closer to her and spoke almost in a whisper, which she was grateful for. "The police are on the line for you. Some detective sergeant from the London Met. She said its urgent."

Kate frowned. She hadn't slept well the night before. She had noticed the two missed calls, and heard the message. She didn't reply, hoping it was a mistake, or a prank call. She got those in the past, and had been the victim of a phone scammer once. But as she looked at Jeff, she knew the truth. She got up and followed him to his office.

"I'll be outside," Jeff said, making for the door.

“Thanks Jeff.” Kate answered the phone. “Kate Turner speaking.”

“Miss Turner, my name is Detective Sergeant Gita Chaudry. We wish to speak to you about a woman called Rachel Mathews. She was your friend, a long time ago.”

As Gita explained, Kate felt her fingers turn to ice, and she gripped the phone like it was falling out of her hand. Her knuckles turned white, and her eyes trembled, the room spinning out of its axis. She blinked, and leaned against the table. The world righted itself, but the spinning remained.

“You found Rachel? In this canal?”

“We found her remains, yes. We understand you were close to her, and gave a statement during the investigation. We would like to speak to you. Is that possible?”

Words, glances, memories kept slipping in and out of the crevices of Kate’s mind like eels. She sat down on a chair.

“Yes, that’s fine.” She thought of the others. Names and faces she’d never forget. Did they know? If the police was calling her, then the others must know.

“Miss Turner?”

“Yes, sorry. I was miles away. This takes me way back, as you can imagine.”

"Of course. We can provide you with more details when we see you. For now, please keep the matter to yourself. Please don't speak to any journalist if they want to get in touch." Gita paused. "Do you stay in touch with your friends from the time when Rachel disappeared?"

Kate wondered where this was heading. "No. They were my university friends, and we kind of lost touch after I got married."

"I see. No problem." Gita cleared her throat. "Do you mind if I ask you a couple of questions now? If you have time, that is."

Kate looked around the office, and outside. Through the glass door and floor to ceiling windows that looked at the open space area, she couldn't see Jeff. He might have gone to the canteen. Maybe if she spoke to the police now, they would leave her alone.

"Sure, go ahead."

"I know this is a long time ago. But did Rachel seem troubled, or worried in the weeks before her disappearance?"

Kate paused, her mind doing a strange dance. "Not that I remember."

"She didn't seem scared to you, or she didn't afraid of anyone?"

Again, Kate felt like she was inside a washing machine, her thoughts rolling around, looking for a way out. But there was no way out. Some ghosts were better off left alone.

"No."

"Did she have a boyfriend, or partner at that time?"

"I'm not sure." Kate desperately tried to recall what she had said in the witness statement, all those years ago. Almost a lifetime ago. She was fifty-three now. "She might have done? I don't remember, sorry. If she did, she didn't tell me the name. Or maybe she did and I don't remember."

Gita paused. Kate wondered if the woman was flicking through her statement from twenty-six years ago as she spoke.

"Thank you. When can we come and see you?"

They agreed on tomorrow, at lunchtime. Kate hung up, putting the phone down on Jeff's desk. She bumped into him as she came out. He was bustling back into his office, striding down the open plan space.

"Come inside," he said. He shut the door behind him, and looked at her inquisitively. "What did they want?"

Jeff used to be an editor for London gossip magazine before he took this job in Kent. A juicy scoop was always at the back of his mind. Journalists loved getting calls from the police. More dirt for them to poke around in.

“It’s a cold case, from many years ago,” Kate opted for the truth, because she knew Jeff would be suspicious. “It was a friend of mine who vanished. They just wanted to ask me about her.”

“Have they reopened the case?”

Kate didn’t want to reveal any details. “Looks like it. She wouldn’t tell me a great deal more. We have to keep this under wraps.” She focused her gaze on Jeff like they were Xray beams. “I mean that.”

Jeff raised both hands. “Hey, this is personal stuff. Off limits, I know. Just wanted to make sure you’re alright.”

“I am. Thank you.”

Kate walked back to her desk. But her mind wasn’t on the review of the hotel in Peru that she was writing. She had visited Peru last year.

She found the office stuffy, and her colleagues sneaking inquisitive looks at her. Or was it her imagination? She got up, suddenly uncomfortable. She took her handbag, and took the lift to the ground floor, and then outside. She took a few deep breaths to calm herself. Times like this, she wished she hadn’t stopped smoking. She went to the garden area in front of the office complex, and sat down on a bench under a tree.

That’s when her phone rang. She stared at the number, not recognising it. A voice inside her told she should answer. Another voice told her to ignore it. But she had the feeling this person would call back again. She answered, wondering if it was actually a reporter who had wind of the news already. But it wasn't a reporter.

"Hi Kate. This is Julia Slater."

Kate opened her mouth to breathe, then let out a shaky sigh. "Julia."

"Yes. Have you heard the news about Rachel?"

"Uh, yes. The police called me."

"We need to talk."

CHAPTER 17

Lisa Moran knocked on Arla's door, and entered. Arla was on a call but she waved her trusted sergeant inside. She finished the call, promising the DI on the line she would interview the constable who had failed his latest performance review – by not turning up to work, and being drunk when he was. The wonders of being a DCI, she thought.

"DI Brian Dempsey is in a nursing home in Croydon. He's got dementia, and doesn't make much sense most days. Potters around the nursing home. I spoke to the manager there. He says Brian is confused about where he is every day. He doesn't recognise anyone. I doubt we'll get much out of him."

Arla stretched her arms upwards, then stood to stretch her back. "What about the DS or DC's in his team?"

"I had better luck there. One of the DC's is now a DI. He works in Hounslow, in the London Met. His name's Quentin Sparrow."

"I want to see him," Arla said. "What about the DS in the team?"

Lisa looked at her notebook. "Mike Boland. He's in his seventies, and retired. He lives at home. I spoke to him. He doesn't remember anything. Refused to talk, basically."

Arla frowned. "We'll see about that. Have you sent him the case files?"

"To both of them, yes. Quentin has agreed to speak to us."

"I want to see Mike Boland first. He would've been senior to Quentin. He might know more about the case."

"He lives near Primrose Hill. I've told him to expect a visit, but he's not happy about it. Said he wants to speak to you first." Lisa's eyes softened, and Arla knew that look. Mike Boland was probably a veteran of the London Met, in the north west sector. He had worked the city's dark corners for most of his life, and Arla owed him a phone call as a professional courtesy, before she visited.

"I'll call him. But get the car ready. I want to see him as well."

After Lisa left, Arla called Mike's number. He didn't answer, and Arla had to try again, this time on the landline. A woman answered.

"Cherie Boland. Who's speaking?"

"DCI Arla Baker from the London Met. Could I please speak to your husband, Mike?"

Cherie was flustered. "Ah…yes, sure. What is this about?"

"Mr Boland will be aware. If I could please speak to him."

After a long pause, a gravelly male voice answered. "Hello. Who is this?"

"Mr Mike Boland?" Arla introduced herself. "My DS sent you the case files of Rachel Mathews?"

"Yes, and I have nothing further to say. I wish you all the best in your investigation. Goodbye."

"We have uncovered new evidence that we would like to ask you about. As the SIO, you would have first-hand knowledge of the case."

Mr Boland wheezed for a few seconds. "What sort of evidence?"

"We can speak when we meet. It's going to be easier."

"Easier? In what way? I told you, I've got nothing to say."

"I think you will find the CCTV evidence interesting, at least. And that's not all. Like I said, it would be easier if we met. I'm happy to come to you."

Mr Boland was quiet for a while. Arla knew what the old man was thinking. He didn't want to get involved in a court battle. This wasn't an open and shut case. In most cold cases the prosecution could carry on for several weeks. But at the same time, Mike also probably knew not talking to Arla would look suspicious.

"Alright then. But not here. I'll meet you at the pub around the corner. It's called the Prince's Arms. Not far from Cricklewood tube stop. Give me a couple of hours."

"Thank you."

Arla hung up, and rang Human Resources. She asked for Boland and Dempsey's files. She knew this would flag up on the system, but there was no harm in that. Within minutes, HR had sent her the folder.

Boland was indeed a veteran of the Met. He had started two years out of school, at the age of eighteen. He worked until he was sixty-eight – seven years ago, when he retired. He worked around Islington for most of his life, but in 2000, he was moved from the Major Investigation Unit, to Community Service Liaison. Arla frowned. That would be a big demotion for a sergeant who was senior enough to become an Inspector – if not a higher rank. She searched through his records, but found nothing.

She looked at Dempsey's file. The older man retired earlier, in 2002. He had taken early retirement at the age of sixty-three. Cross referencing with Boland's file, Arla saw that the two men had worked together for a number of years. She found an interesting fact. Just before his retirement, in 2000, Dempsey and Boland had led the prosecution of an East End gangster boss called Richard McPherson. The charges didn't stick, and McPherson went off free. His Organised Crime Network, or OCN, was the largest in London at the time.

Working quickly, Arla checked the trial notes. She needed to know Dempsey and Boland better. In the trial notes, she read the police were accused of corruption, and hiding evidence, and also of planting false evidence. They were baseless allegations, and no evidence was found. But the dreaded Anti Corruption Unit, or ACU, had investigated Dempsey and Boland. And they found nothing.

Arla looked back through the files of a selection of the other cases both men had been involved in. They ranged from armed robbery to murders, including the disappearance of Rachel Mathews. No other accusations of corruption were levelled at the two men. Arla did notice one thing though. One the basis of the cases she saw – Dempsey's prosecution rate was abysmal. It was 0.3, which mean for every ten cases he brought to trial, he only succeeded in three. In other words, seven out of ten times, the criminals went free.

Not a great record. Arla's own record was 0.98, which meant she put a criminal behind bar for most of the cases she handled. 0.3 was low enough for Arla to wonder if Dempsey should've been retired longer ago.

Her phone beeped, and it was a text message from Nicole. She was enjoying herself on her trip, and had sent her a photo of surfing with her friends.

Arla replied back, then went out to the open plan office. Lisa and Rob were at their desks. Lisa got up and put her coat on.

"Gita and Ros have gone to see Julia Slater," Rob said. "I'll chase up Dr Banerjee and Parmentier to see what they have."

"Good. And also check to see if we can get hold of any more CCTV from 1998." Arla put a hand on her waist as she remembered. "That man we saw speaking to Rachel, any sign of him?"

Lisa answered. "No facial recognition software match on our databases, or on HOLMES. So, no ID as yet. Rachel's friends didn't mention this guy, but the girls have taken his photo when they went to meet Julia. And Melissa later on today."

"Alright. We need to find out who that man was. It's possible Rachel kept it a secret from her friends, for whatever reason. It could be the breakthrough we need."

Waving goodbye at Rob, Arla followed Lisa out to the rear car park. She called Harry on the way. He didn't answer, which meant he was on the firing range. Lisa took the wheels of the black BMW, and pointed its nose through the London traffic to head up north.

"Let's take the tube," Arla suggested, when they were stuck in traffic on Clapham High Street. Lisa pulled over and parked. They had the option of putting the siren on to get through the traffic, but they couldn't do that all the way. And taking the tube was the quickest way around London.

They were rattling along in one of the trains when Lisa leaned over to Arla. "Why do you think Boland wants to meet us in the pub?"

"Nosey wife?"

"Got to be more than that. They're both retired so always in each other's faces. They must be used to it by now. Perhaps we should speak to the wife separately."

"That's what I was thinking. There's clearly something he doesn't want to discuss in front of his wife."

"Yes. But he also wants to meet in a public place. With CCTV cameras. He's worried."

"About what?"

Arla winked at Lisa. "We'll find out soon enough."

It didn't take them long to get to the pub from Cricklewood station. Boland had been right about the directions. Arla spotted him as soon as they walked in to the main bar. It was one of those old school London pubs – stained glass windows with green, blue and red floral patterns, framed paintings of all sizes on the dark wood panelled walls. The mahogany bar counter shone in the mid morning light that cascaded in through the windows.

A few punters were nursing their morning pints, and they were a minority. The majority of the seats were empty, and the old man sat in the corner seat on the right was unmistakable as an ex-copper. He was positioned in the right spot to see who came in, and Arla could see a side exit a few metres away from his table. The man had a bald head, wrinkles on his face so deep that his forehead looked like an army of caterpillars had made it their home. His grey eyes were sharp behind the glasses. He was staring directly at them. A half pint of coke rested on the table.

Arla and Lisa walked up to him. "Mike Boland?" Arla asked. The man nodded, and Arla showed her warrant card. He inspected it with interest.

"Not hard to recognize your own kind, eh?" Boland said. His hirsute eyebrows joined the layers of wrinkles to move up and down like a rainforest in a storm.

His keen eyes wandered over Arla's face, then switched to Lisa, before returning to Arla again.

“What do you want to know? That girl’s disappearance was a long time ago. Is she the body they found in Regent’s Canal?”

“Yes.” Arla glanced at Lisa, who took out the tablet device. She played the CCTV footage of Rachel with the man, and handed it to Boland.

Arla watched the old man as his freckled and spotted bald head lowered to look at the screen.

“That man was seen with the victim, and your team did not act on this CCTV footage. Why?”

“Victim?” Boland lifted his head slowly. “You think she was killed?”

“We’re keeping our options open. Tell us, please. What happened to the evidence?” Arla pointed at the screen. “There’s no mention of it in the SIO’s reports.”

“You better ask him then,” Boland said, pushing the tablet away. “I’ve never seen this.”

“And you remember the case, obviously?”

“Yes. You sent me the file again, anyway. Look, what’s this about?”

Arla ignored his question. “A neighbour also saw a man in a Porsche who dropped Rachel back home, late at night. Twice, over a three week period. Your team didn’t act on this information – according to the report.”

“Again, I’m not sure why you’re asking me about something that happened almost thirty years ago.”

If he was any more evasive, Arla thought, the man might disappear in a puff of smoke. She hooked eyes with him, and kept her voice low.

“Your team, of which you were a senior member, ignored important evidence which should’ve been acted on. I am the SIO now, and I need to know why. Brian Dempsey has advanced dementia, he cannot help. We will meet one of the DC’s who worked with you. But after Dempsey, you were the most senior member of the team.”

“I didn’t get a medal for it,” the smile was like a rabid dog baring its teeth. “You want me to solve your case for you? Sorry, not in that line of work. Not anymore, anyway.”

“You were investigated by the ACU. They found nothing. But then you were demoted to Uniforms, and you worked in Crowd Control for the last seven years of your career. Why was that?”

“I needed a change of scenery,” Boland said, like he was discussing the weather. “Not a crime, is it?”

“So you asked for it? Or were you pushed?”

“I asked for it,” Boland grinned like a hyena again.

“You’re worried. Your feet are tapping, and your hands keep moving. You wanted to meet us here because you didn’t trust we were police, or the right kind of police. You wanted a public place so there would be witnesses and cameras."

That sliced through his armour, and he blinked several times. He recovered quickly. "You've never met a colleague in the pub before? Or is it all changed nowadays? Will I get arrested for calling you love, or sweetheart?

Arla and Lisa exchanged a glance. Boland was one of the sexist dinosaurs who had been weeded out of the police force. Clearly, he wasn't afraid to still show his true colours.

Arla turned her dead cold eyes on him. "Do you remember Richard Mcpherson?"

The words hit home. The wrinkles on the forehead cleared for an instant, before slowly bunching back up like a piece of paper getting folded from either end.

"You and Dempsey dealt with his case, but he got off free, didn't he?"

"So what? That man got arrested several times. He did finally go down."

"But not by your hands." Arla put her elbows on the table. "What happened to you, Mike? Why did you lose your job as a detective?"

"And why are you so worried that you wouldn't meet us at your house?" Lisa added. "Not concerned about a hit, are you?"

Slowly, Boland turned to look at Lisa. She said, "You wouldn't be the first copper who was on the take. Were you pals with McPherson? Did you get found out?"

Boland reached for his hat. Arla raised a hand, and he stopped for a fraction of a second. Then calmly, he got his hat and put it on his head.

"Tell us about the Rachel Mathews case. Why was this evidence not looked at?"

"I don't know. You're asking the wrong person. Dempsey was the SIO."

"And it's convenient he can't say anything, isn't it?"

Boland pulled the hat lower over his face, and got to his feet. His joints creaked, and the knees popped. His grizzly, gaunt face looked white and colourless. He looked like a man with a death sentence, and that worried Arla.

He stretched to his full height. His back had a gentle stoop, and he wasn't a tall man. His eyes were dull behind the black frame glasses.

"There's a saying, DCI Baker. If you dig for an earthworm, you end up with a snake."

"Remember what I said. If I were you, I'd let this go. That girl died by suicide. That's all there is to it."

Arla and Lisa watched from their seats as Boland shuffled down the tiled floor, heading for the door.

CHAPTER 18

"We can't get him, guv, can we?" Lisa asked, when they stepped outside the pub. She was referring to Boland. "He was cleared by the ACU. And so was Dempsey."

"Yes." Arla walked with head bent, observing the pavement stones. "But they neglected to follow up crucial evidence. Boland knows that. He's worried. Actually," she grinned. "I know someone who might help."

She called Harry, who answered this time. "Sorry missed your call. I was in the shooting range."

"You might be able to help with something. Remember that East End crime family you did surveillance on last year?"

"The Fagan Boys OCN? Yes, what about them?"

"Well, do you still have the informer's details? We might need to set up a meeting with him."

"Yes, I do have it somewhere. What's this about?"

Arla told him. Harry sounded thoughtful. “Why do you think there’s an OCN link?”

“Boland and Dempsey were involved in the McPherson case, and that man ran a huge OCN in the 1990s.”

“Yes, I remember McPherson. Alright. Let me reach out and see if this guy is still around. We have to be cautious though. He put his life at risk to rat on his boss, and we gave him a name change and witness protection. I need to find his new details.”

“No worries. See you back at the nick.”

By the time they got back to Clapham, Harry had also arrived. Arla was relieved to see him. He had only been practising on the range, and she knew it was irrational to think he was on an operation, getting shot at. That was her worst nightmare. Harry was enjoying himself, and she didn’t know how to deal with it. She didn’t want to stop him, but she knew sooner rather than later, Harry would be a certified AFO. She wasn’t looking forward to that day.

Harry was at his desk, next to Rob, who was standing behind him, and both men were staring at the laptop screen on Harry’s desk.

Harry tore his eyes off the screen as Arla appeared. “Rob’s just brought me up to speed. We’re looking for that young man who was seen with Rachel Mathews, aren’t we?”

"You've got your skates on," Arla said approvingly.

"That's me. Mr Swift," Harry grinned. "Not to mention efficient."

"Or big headed," Arla rolled her eyes. "Stop talking and show me what you've got."

"How can a man refuse an offer like that?" Harry nudged Rob, who laughed.

Arla stood next to Harry and peered at the screen. A black and white CCTV image was divided into four boxes. The date was 10th October 1998.

Rob said, "We didn't find any more CCTV footage of Rachel. But Harry had the bright idea of looking for footage of the young man with her. So I spoke to Traffic, and they did a facial recognition search for him, on CCTV from 1998. This is what we came up with."

Arla wanted to say well done, but she didn't want to give Harry any more compliments. If his ego was any more inflated the man might swell up like a balloon and float away. The image of a swollen Harry ascending into the sky amused her. She might save it for later, to bring him down a peg or two. Harry the flying pig. Great vision of a police officer. *Hee hee.*

She clapped a hand on his admittedly broad shoulder. "Go on then. Play it, Harry."

"Sounds like a famous line from a film. Alright then Your Majesty."

They watched the screen as the man walked down the street. It was in Hoxton Square, the address was written on the top right corner, next to the date and time. They watched as the man walked around, then went inside a park. He sat down on a bench and started reading a book.

"He doesn't look like Terry Smith, does he?" Lisa asked, staring at the screen.

"No," Arla shook her head.

Arla knew this man's face had not shown a match on any of the police databases, or on HOLMES – the supercomputer in Whitehall, which had data from all over the world. Which meant he wasn't a criminal or terrorist. But all that signified was that he had never been arrested. Regardless, she was now stuck. It would be a nightmare to get this man's identity….unless…

"Have you searched for his face in more recent years?" Arla asked.

"Yes," Rob answered. "We found a match three years later, in 2001. It was in Dover, Kent. Presumably he had moved there."

"And two years later," Harry said, "In 2006, he was back in London. Let's check that, as I haven't seen it yet."

He clicked on the keyboard, and the man's image appeared on the lower right box of the divided screen.

They followed the man as he walked on the high street, and then got on a bus.

"We need his identity. This man has moved around. He might well have something to hide."

Lisa shook her head. "That's going to be a pin in a haystack, guv. If this guy's not been caught doing something, even a speeding ticket, he doesn't exist on our systems."

"And so far, we have nothing on him." Rob added.

Arla said, "Zoom in on his face."

Harry did as told. Arla saw a lean, long face, with a slender nose that fitted well with his long features. His slate grey eyes were large, and he had a flop of dark hair that fell over his forehead. His cheekbones were high, and the lips full, with an intense look in his black eyes. Darkly attractive, Arla thought, with a hint of danger in those eyes.

Arla crossed her arms across her chest, and tapped a finger against her elbow. The best looking men turned out to be the most evil at time – in her experience. She needed to find this man quickly. If he was responsible for Rachel's death – what else had he done all these years? The thought made her skin crawl.

"Follow him," she said, "to see if he goes into a shop or business from where we might be able to get customer data."

It was 2006 on the screen now, and Arla knew CCTV was wide spread by then. Harry nodded, and sped up the tape. The man was now identified by a red circle around his head. The location was back in Hoxton Square, back where the man was seen three years ago. Hoxton Square was close to Islington, where Rachel had lived.

Harry stopped the tape suddenly. He pointed to the upper right box, and Arla saw what Harry was examining. The man had been stopped by a policeman, in front of a car. It seemed the car belonged to the man, and he had parked illegally. Harry zoomed in on the car, after the man got inside. He copied and cut the car's registration number, and posted it on the DVLA website.

The car did not exist anymore. But Harry checked the historical records, and found a match with the registration number. There was a form called the V888, which listed all of the vehicle's previous owner. A list of them came up. Between 2005 and 2010, the car was owned by a man called Simon Barnaby.

"Aren't I clever," Harry craned his head backward to look at Arla, and winked. Then he searched for the name on the DVLA website again and found the man's driving licence photocard.

All of them leaned forward as the image appeared on the screen. "That's him," Arla said, her eyes shining. She gripped Harry's shoulder, and wanted to kiss his head, but knew it would be inappropriate. Excitement rolled in her veins.

"You do have your uses, DI Mehta," she said to Harry. "Sometimes."

"Oh, you know me. I aim to please." Harry stood, towering above everyone else. He yawned and stretched his hands upward, cracking his wrist joints.

Arla turned to the others. "Find out where this man is now. If he doesn't want to talk, arrest him and bring him here."

CHAPTER 19

Ros May and Gita Chaudry came up from the tube stop at Sloane Square. It was warm, and the pedestrians and cars made the heat congealed, caged between the lovely red brick buildings. Chelsea and Sloane Square were the epitome of London's fashionable hot spots. Lamborghinis and Ferrari's growled at being held up in traffic, like mechanical beasts voicing their hunger.

Ros stopped to look inside a boutique and pointed at a handbag. "That's what I want. Not for work of course, but when I'm going out."

Gita nodded, as if she was absent minded. They carried on walking. Julia Slater's office was a ten minute walk.

"Are you alright?" Ros asked a few minutes later. Gita looked at her and nodded in silence again. Ros waited for her to speak. She had worked with Gita for three years now and got to know her well. They had been to each other's houses. And Ros knew Gita's now ex-partner – Mark. She also knew how much the break up had affected Gita. Twelve years was a long time to be with someone.

They walked past a coffee shop, and Ros asked Gita if she wanted one, and she agreed. They got their coffees and sat down at a roadside table.

Ros said, “I’m worried about you.”

Gita smiled, but it was sad, and there was no sparkle in her flat eyes. “Don’t be. I’m dealing with it, and it’s just a matter of getting used to it.”

“Has Mark moved all his stuff out now? Or does he come back every now and then?”

“He has, but we’re still sharing a car. So I see him about that. The flat is on the market, but selling it’s been a nightmare. Lots of viewings, but no one wants to buy it.”

“I’m sure it will sell soon. You shouldn’t have to drop the price. It’s a nice flat, in a great location.”

“That’s what I thought. But I’ve got a feeling Mark has agreed with the agents to price it high. That’s why its not selling.” Gita flexed her jaws once and sighed. “I want to get out of there. The sooner the better. But at this rate, it will take ages. That’s what I don’t want.”

Ros patted Gita’s hand. She knew Gita felt trapped. She had been in this situation once, but she and her boyfriend were renting. It was easy to move out.

"What about your parents? Could you stay there for a while?" Ros knew Gita's parents lived in Guildford, a Surrey town not far from Wimbledon, where Gita lived.

Gita downturned her lips. "I could, but I can't cope with living with my mum. She's full of advice these days, and wants me to meet these guys that her friends know. Well, the sons or relatives of her friends. It's the worst thing for me right now – to think about meeting someone."

Ros couldn't help but smile. "Is your mum pushy?"

"Like you wouldn't believe. She'd move in with me right now, just to make sure," Gita raised both hands to make quotation marks in the air, "That I was well supported. Apparently, I can't look after myself."

"Does she have a point?"

"What? No." Gita frowned. "Look, I'm alright, honestly. The truth is Mark wants to find a younger woman and start a family. I'm forty next year."

"You can still have a child," Ros said gently. "These days women are having children into their forties."

Gita shook her head, and a veil of sadness slipped over her face like a bank of clouds over the sun.

"My time for starting a family has gone. We did try." She glanced at Ros, and looked away.

"I know. I'm sorry." Three years ago, Gita had a number of miscarriages. Ros worried that she hadn't really recovered from that, and it had fatally damaged her relationship.

"Life goes on, Geets. You know that, hon, don't you?"

"Yes, I do." Gita flexed her jaws again, and the sadness rose into her eyes. She didn't quite blink back the tears. She had got used to this new life, or so she thought.

"I'm moving on," she said. "I just need to get used to being on my own. And to be honest, its not that bad."

"That's the spirit," Ros smiled. "Why don't we go out this weekend? We can go for a drink in town, and then see what happens."

Gita grinned back. "I'd like that."

They finished their coffees, and then walked to Cadogan Square. The receptionist at the desk told them to take a seat, then left her own and vanished through a door behind a book shelf. She returned soon, and waved them over. Then she led them down a corridor, and into another office reception space. She knocked on a door that had Julia Slater's name and title of Counsellor.

The door opened, and Ros saw a woman in a charcoal grey trouser suit, with grey heels to match. Her hair was tied back in a ponytail. She had mascara under her eyes, and she looked tired, like she'd just been doing something stressful, and for too long. Perhaps the mascara was to hide the shadows under her eyes, Ros thought. She showed her warrant card, along with Gita.

"I spoke to you on the phone," Gita said. "May we come in please?"

"Yes, of course," Julia gave them a tight smile, and held the door open for them. Then she shut and locked it. They were in a spacious office, nicely decorated with house plants and potted flowers. Julia Slater's degree certificate hung on the wall above the desk. There was a couch for her clients, and armchairs around it, with a coffee table in the middle. Julia sat behind her desk, and the detectives took their place in the armchairs.

"Thank you for seeing us," Gita began. "We know this must be a shock to you. I know this was a long time ago. How well did you know Rachel?"

Julia cleared her throat. "We went to the same university, and lived together for a while in student accommodation. So I got to know her quite well."

"What was Rachel like as a person? And did she seem alright to you in the days and weeks before she disappeared?"

Julia shrugged. "She was quiet. She kept to herself, unless she was with her close friends. Then she could be loud." Julia smiled at the memory.

“We know that she suffered with depression. Did that affect her life much?”

Julia seemed on the verge of saying something, but then changed her mind. She nodded, and her face was grave.

“Yes, it did. She could be prone to it. She took medications on and off, but not regularly.”

“And she wasn’t prescribed any medications for about a year before she disappeared, was she?”

“Maybe,” Julia shrugged. “I didn’t see her take any, if that’s what you wanted to know.”

There was a note of impatience in her voice, as if she wanted to get this over and done with as soon as possible. Perhaps she was having a bad day. Or maybe it was something else.

Ros glanced at Gita, and she knew her colleague had also felt it. Gita said, “When did you last see Rachel?”

“It had been a while, to be honest. We normally met up every couple of weeks. But we both had work, and she had other friends, I guess. We were close, but we also had our own lives. I hadn’t seen her for three weeks. I called and texted her but got no response. I was driving past her house one evening and decided to stop and knock on her door. She didn’t answer, and her neighbours said they hadn’t seen her for a couple of days. That’s when I got worried.”

"What did you do?"

"I didn't have her mother's phone number. I thought she might have gone up north. But then I saw her mother, when I went back to her flat. That's when I knew something was wrong. I reported her missing that day. Her mother, Sarah, had already done so."

They were silent for a few seconds. Gita exchanged a quick look with Rita. So far, Julia had stuck to the events in her statement.

Ros took over. "Did you know Rachel's boyfriends?"

"I met Terry Smith, her partner, before he left for Australia. They broke up almost a year before Rachel went missing."

"And she didn't date any other men after?"

"Not that I knew of," Julia was staring at Ros, who let the silence prolong for a few seconds. Julia fidgeted. Her hands moved on the desk, and she shifted in her seat.

"Did you ask her?"

Julia retained a blank face, but Ros thought it was an effort. Julia's breathing was slightly more laboured.

"This was a long time ago, Detective. No, I don't remember asking her. Like I said, we did have our own lives as well. We didn't know everything about each other."

“It’s just that girlfriends talk about these kind of things, don’t they?” Ros waved a hand. “If Rachel had a new man in her life, why would she keep it a secret from her closest friend?”

Julia shrugged. The effort remained on her face. She was trying too hard to be relaxed, and it wasn’t working.

“I’m not sure if I was her closest friend.”

“Yes, we are speaking to Melissa Carrington, and Kate Turner as well. They didn’t mention a new partner in her life. If Julia had a man, do you really think she would keep that secret from all three of you?

“Maybe she didn’t have to. If she didn’t have a man in her life, then why would she bother?”

Julia attempted a smile. It didn’t touch her eyes. Gita asked, “Was Rachel closer to you, or to Melissa and Kate?”

Julia down turned her lips, and was thoughtful. “That’s a difficult one to answer. I talked to her a lot, but I know she also spoke to Kate. She was closer to Kate and myself than she was to Melissa.”

Ros flicked her eyes at Gita, who caught the meaning. She took out her phone, where she had stored an image of the man on CCTV – Simon Barnaby. It was a close up of his face, on his driving licence.

“Have you seen this man before?”

Julia leaned over, and Gita stood and walked over to her desk. She handed Julia the phone, who looked at the screen closely.

"Can't say that I have," Julia said slowly. She gave the phone back to Gita. "Who is he?"

Gita focused on Julia, watching her face and neck muscles. Her hands were relaxed, and her body was still. Gita didn't think Julia was lying about this.

"He was seen with Rachel in the days before she disappeared. Outside a pub, and near the tube stop at her work. We tracked him across a few locations. He seemed to be living in Islington. That's where Rachel lived."

"Near Angel, yes. No, I've never seen this man." Julia glanced from Gita to Ros. "Was he dating Rachel? Is that why you're…

"Yes," Ros said, as Gita went back to her chair. "We think they were dating in any case. They were holding hands, and standing close to each other. It seems they were together."

A thin, humourless smile appeared on Julia's lips. "So that's why you were so keen on finding out if I knew about Rachel's love life. Well, like I said, she didn't tell me everything."

"It's a little strange, that's all. You knew Terry. You must've known her previous partners as well."

"That's true, I did. So did Mel and Kate. Maybe Rachel was waiting for the right moment to introduce him to us?"

"Perhaps." Ros saw that Julia seemed a little brighter now. And also a little smug.

Ros asked, "This is a personal question. I hope you don't mind me. Did Rachel discuss her sexual preferences or habits with you?"

Julia blinked a few times. "Well, we talked about it, yes. Like friends do. What about it?"

Julia glared at Gita for a few beats, then looked at the watch on her left wrist.

"Now, if you'll excuse me, I have a client waiting."

Ros and Gita exchanged a glance, checking if there was anything else they wanted to cover. Then they rose, and Ros handed her card across the table. Julia accepted it.

"If you remember anything else please give us a call. We are treating Rachel's death as suspicious. It wasn't a suicide, as previously assumed. She wouldn't be rolled up in a tarpaulin with stones tied to it, if it was a suicide." Ros paused, and stared directly at Julia.

"Rachel was killed."

Julia's jaws flexed once, and the corners of her eyes constricted. "I understand. Yes, I will call you if I recall anything else."

“Thank you.”

At the door, Gita turned, her hand on the handle. “By the way. Did you call any of your friends to talk about this? I mean Melissa or Kate.” Gita relaxed her expression. “It’s okay if you have.”

Julia stared at her for a moment, then shook her head. “No. I haven’t.”

CHAPTER 20

Arla and Harry had driven to Slough. It was past five pm, and the roads were getting busy with traffic. Clouds had scudded over the sky, and it was getting dark and overcast. Slough was an industrial town, about twenty miles to the north west from central London. Harry followed directions on his satnav to a housing estate outside the city centre.

The wide avenues of the main centre narrowed into streets of terraced houses, and they came into a complex of council houses – tall grey cement towers that housed the dredges of society.

"Looks familiar," Harry remarked. Arla had to agree. The Clapham Police Station was built adjacent to a similar council estate. Harry drove down slowly past the giant towers, to a row of terraced homes in a cul de sac. Graffiti adorned the walls in places, but despite being council owned, the street was clean, and there was no sign of uncollected rubbish, or burn out cars.

"He's definitely at home?" Arla asked, when they stopped outside number thirty-two. Rain had arrived, pelting the windscreen. Harry turned the wipers on, and they both squinted across the street in the sudden down pour.

"He said he would be when I spoke to him. Let's see."

They got out, and Arla ran across the road, and sheltered under the porch. Harry followed sedately, the rain not bothering him. Arla pressed the buzzer and they waited. It was a simple, two up and two down terraced house, like most of the others in the cul de sac. It had seen better days. Patches of damp spread under one of the windows, and the white paint had long ago turned to a sordid grey, mirroring the sky.

A woman opened the door, holding a baby on her lap. The toddler squirmed, but then was captivated by the strangers. Arla thought it was a boy. He stared at them with large, round blue eyes.

"DI Mehta from the London Met," Harry said. "Is Brian in?"

The woman, who was young, and no more than in her early thirties, looked at Harry suspiciously.

"No, he ain't. What do you want?"

"I called him to speak about a police matter. He said he was going to be at home."

"Well, he's not though, is he? And I don't know where he's gone."

"When did he leave?"

The woman shrugged. The baby squirmed in her lap again, and she bounced him a couple of times.

"About an hour ago. I was busy with the little one upstairs. I heard the front door shut. He didn't say where he was going. I thought he was going out to the shops."

Arla said, "You didn't call him? It's been an hour."

The woman looked at Arla as if she had grown two heads, and was speaking in a language she didn't understand.

"'Course I called him. He didn't answer. Then he sent a text to say he's meeting up with a couple of mates and he'll be back soon."

"Where do you think he might be?"

The woman shrugged again. The boy was restless now, and she had to put him on the floor. He was unsteady on his feet, but still keen to walk. He took a few steps, fell down and got back up again. The woman looked up at them.

"Look, I'm busy and that, alright? He's told me nothin' about you lot comin'. Can you just call him and sort it out, yeah?"

Arla didn't think the woman was lying. Harry nodded, looking frustrated, and pulled out his phone. The woman shut the door. The rain was still pelting down, splattering on the pavement. Puddles were forming on the road.

Harry left a message and hung up. "He's not answering."

Arla pressed on the buzzer again, and the woman answered, her face flushed. She put a hand on her waist, and glared at Arla. The boy trundled up behind her, and grabbed her leg. Then he stuck his tongue out at them, and pointed at Harry.

"What is it now?" The woman demanded.

"What's his local pub? Or bar?" Arla said.

"There's one around the corner, about ten minutes walk. He goes there normally. There's some shops on the parade as well. Have a look there." Her eyes shot daggers at her and Harry.

"Can you lot just leave me alone now?"

"What's the pub called?"

"The King's Head."

"Thanks and sorry to bother you," Arla said. The woman shut the door for the second time. They got back in the car. Harry had an umbrella in the back, but Arla didn't want to walk in the rain. It was still chucking it down.

Harry parked outside the pub in the corner. The sign that proclaimed its name had listed to one side. The black and white Victorian wood work front was well preserved, and in the gloom that had now pervaded the skies, yellow lights glowed in the windows. On the first floor, lights also glowed in some of the windows. Further along, a small supermarket, and a corner shop stood next to a betting shop and a pawnbroker. Boarded up shop windows followed after that. In the steady drum of rain, the street was deserted. Some people huddled under a bus shelter.

Harry parked, and they got out, and ran across the street. Harry held the door open for Arla. A bar tender looked up, and so did a few of the punters. The bubble of conversation faded for a few seconds. Then the heads turned back to their pints. Harry walked up to the bar with Arla. The bar tender was tall and wide, with a handle bar moustache. He had tattoos all the way up his elbows, vanishing under his sleeves. His half sleeve black leather jacket, and leather trousers suggested to Arla he might be a biker. His cold, unfriendly eyes suggested to Arla he knew they were cops.

“We’re looking for Brian Copeland. Have you seen him?”

The biker bartender shook his head slowly, keeping his eyes on Harry. “Medium height, short dark hair,” Harry said. “He lives around the corner and he drinks here. Are you sure you haven’t seen him?”

Arla looked around the pub. The interior was cosy, with varnished pine wood panelling, dark red carpet on the floor. It wasn't a high-end establishment, more a drinking hole for local people than a gastro pub. The hard faced, unfriendly looks directed at Arla and Harry didn't bode particularly well. But Arla was used to it. She received the same treatment when she turned up at a pub asking for one of the locals.

"Lots come and go from here, mate," the bar tender said calmly. "I don't keep tabs."

"You've got CCTV, right?" Harry indicated the camera behind the bartender's head.

The biker sighed. "Yes, and so? There's not been any trouble. What do you need to see this man for?"

"A police matter," Harry said blandly. "When was Brian last here?"

"Like I said, I don't know." The man made a show of wiping the bar, and moved away. Harry muttered under his breath.

"Let's have a look around," Harry suggested. Arla nodded, and they walked slowly down the pub, Harry casting an eye around carefully. He didn't see Brian, and every face his eyes met looked away quickly. They got to the other end of the bar, and saw the swing doors for the exit. Harry turned, stuffed his hands in his coat pocket, and rocked on his heels as he looked around the bar. No one looked at him.

“Let’s go,” Arla said. Harry maintained his position for a few seconds, then turned and followed Arla. The rain had subsided to a drizzle, thankfully. Arla ran across the street to the car. She was about to get in the car, when Harry caught her arm.

“Let’s walk this way,” he whispered. Arla didn’t ask why. Brian was Harry’s contact, and he knew what to do. She walked with him, and he turned into a side alley opposite the pub. They stood in a corner, and Harry watched the pub’s entrance.

“You found someone?” Arla whispered. A car zipped past on the road. Thunder rumbled in the sky, and the gloom had deepened. A storm was on its way.

“Maybe. Let’s wait.” He looked up. “Glad the rain stopped. But it might start again.”

Arla snuggled close to Harry, and she could tell he wanted to put his arm around her. But that wouldn’t be very professional, as they were on duty. She could feel him tense, his muscles taut as he stared at the pub.

After a few slow minutes had passed, a man emerged from the entrance they had left. He was short, and he wore a black bomber jacket and dark jeans, a baseball cap pulled over his face. He lit a cigarette, and then looked around.

“Stay here,” Harry said. “Don’t follow me.”

Arla watched as Harry stepped out of the alley, and leaned against the wall. The man opposite saw him. A silent message passed between them. The man stubbed his cigarette out on the pavement, and kicked it to the gutter. Then he walked past Harry, and away from him. Harry waited a beat, then followed.

CHAPTER 21

Harry walked slowly as he didn't want to attract attention. He had long legs on his six feet four inch frame, and unlike any of the pedestrians he passed, he wore a suit. He caught the look on their eyes, appraising him silently as they walked past. The man in the baseball cap had walked ahead quickly, and Harry couldn't see him. He didn't have much choice but to speed up.

He saw the man emerge from behind a bus station. He glanced around him briefly, and he saw Harry. He started walking fast again, and Harry followed. The man took a right turn and vanished from view. Harry quickened his pace, and saw the man hurrying ahead. A little knot of concern was tightening in Harry's mind. If this man wanted to speak to him, why was he rushing ahead?

Harry was used to informers. They were mostly criminals who had evidence against them and wanted to cut a deal with the police for a lighter sentences, or the gang they worked for had turned against them. Or threatened their families. Informers tended to be nervous. Maybe that's why this man was acting like he was trying to run away from Harry. But Harry knew his type. He wanted to talk.

The man stopped at the mouth of an alley, and looked behind him, as if to make sure Harry was still there. Then he ducked inside the alley and vanished again. Swearing, Harry sped up, now casting caution to the wind. He wanted to run, but instead, walked faster. He was out of breath when he got to the alley. It was a narrow space between the gardens of two rows of houses. The walls on either end were two metres high, and he could see over the edges. Gardens of terraced houses stood on either side. He couldn't see the man anymore.

Harry broke into a run. A flicker of movement caught his eyes. A shadow appeared over a wall to his right, and a man jumped over. To his left, another did the same. Harry skidded to a halt. The two men stood there, black hoods pulled over their heads. Harry wished he had his firearm. He was allowed to carry it around when he was on duty. But foolishly, he had left his weapon on the range.

One of the men saw him put his hand inside his coat. His hand also dived in his jeans. He lifted his gun partially, to show Harry the grey metallic butt of the weapon.

"We got shrapnel too, Mr Pig. Don't do it. Show me your hands."

Harry took his hand out slowly and raised them. These men were serious. The two men stepped forward. Harry heard a sound and turned behind. Two men had appeared behind him as well. He was trapped.

The man with the gun seemed to be the leader. He stopped a few feet away from Harry. His cold eyes looked Harry up and down. His face was devoid of expression.

"Why are you asking about McPherson?"

So, Brian had talked. Or someone was tapping his phone. Either way, word had spread. Harry wondered if Brian was still alive.

Harry said nothing. The man angled his head. The hoodie remained, obscuring his features. He had a light ginger beard, and his eyes gleamed at Harry.

"Not going to talk, DI Mehta?"

Harry was surprised, and the man saw it. A nasty smile appeared on his lips. "Oh, we know a lot about you. Bust up the Fagan boys in the East End, dinnya? Think you're the dogs bollocks, eh?"

The smiled vanished as the man straightened. "But what do you want from Mr Mcpherson?"

Harry shrugged. "Just to say hello. Ask him how he is."

“Shut up,” the man ground out. His hand snaked into his trouser pocket again and Harry saw him grip the butt of his gun.

“I’ve got a silencer. I could kill you right here if you don’t tell me.”

“I’ve got nothing to say about McPherson.”

The man’s unblinking eyes stared at Harry. This man was a senior member of McPherson’s gang, or else he wouldn’t have the sort of clout needed to tap a phone, or speak to Brian – who was living under a fake name and identity. The concern in Harry’s mind was now a raging flame. Something much deeper was going on here, and he couldn’t understand it.

“You lot have spoken to one of the old cops. Mike Boland. What for?”

“Something else.”

“Why don’t you tell me?”

Harry suspected the man knew already. But he was playing his cards close to his chest. Had he, or Mcpherson, spoken to Boland? Is this what Boland meant when he told Arla not to dig around?

If Harry told him the truth, he wasn’t giving much away. It was in the papers already. “A dead body in Regent’s Canal. Boland and his boss Dempsey dealt with the case many years ago.”

“And what have you found so far?”

Harry shrugged again, and exhaled. "You, actually. Why don't tell me what you know about the case? Why are you so concerned?"

"I'm asking the questions," the man said quietly.

"Shall we go inside and talk? It might start raining soon. You lot have hoodies on, but my hair gel might start to run."

"You should've been a comedian. Being a copper's wasted on yer."

The man came forward, within touching distance. His eyes flashed and Harry braced himself. But the man didn't move a muscle. Instead, Harry felt movement behind him, and before he could shift, a sharp crack resounded across the back of his skull. A red orange fireball of pain exploded across his head, and the sky turned upside down, the houses rising up as if they were floating in the air. Another blow to the back of his head, and his eyes dimmed, turning black. Harry stumbled, and fell to his knees.

"Tell us what you know so far. How did that girl die?"

Harry could barely speak. His head was spinning, and nausea rose up in his throat. But he managed a few words.

"Why don't you tell me?"

"Last chance."

"Tell Mr McPherson he made a mistake."

Harry felt something slip across his throat, and he knew it was rope. It tightened across his throat, and his neck jerked back. Harry dug his fingers into the rope, desperately trying to loosen the stranglehold.

"Goodbye DI Mehta." The man turned on his heels and left with his accomplice. But the two men behind Harry remained. Harry managed to get his fingers down the rope, grabbed it as tightly as he could, then kicked back with one leg. He caught the man's legs and he slipped. Harry bent forward, pulling the man over him. The man resisted, but Harry tumbled on the ground, and the man lost his balance. His friend came around the side, and kicked Harry in the head.

Pain spread in Harry's skull like a malignant mushroom. Blows rained down on him, and somehow he got to his feet and moved away, crashing against the side wall. But the two men followed, kicking and punching. Then he felt the cold barrel of a weapon against his skull.

"Finish it," a voice said. Harry heard the hammer being drawn back, and the safety released. Was it going to end like this? In a shit hole street in Slough, of all the bloody places? Nicole and Arla's face swam in his eyes, and he murmured a goodbye to them. Then his eyes closed.

"Stop," a voice rang out behind them. Harry felt the gun move away from his face. The knee pressed on his chest also moved, and he sucked in a deep breath.

He forced his eyes open, and saw Arla, standing there with a Taser in her hand.

"You're surrounded," Arla shouted. "Backup is arriving soon. Throw your weapon down." Harry heard the whine of sirens then, getting loud very quickly. The two men turned and ran for it. Arla crouched by Harry, helping him to sit up.

Concern masked her face. "Are you alright?" She touched his head and he grimaced.

"Ow. Not there." He looked down at his white shirt now splattered with blood. "That was a Ralph Lauren shirt, damn it. What a waste."

CHAPTER 22

Harry had a bandage around his head, and he needed three stitches on the side of his scalp. He was in the hospital bed, feeling groggy from the pain killers. The doctors had gone, and he was alone with Arla.

"Who says drugs don't work?" He smiled at her. "I feel high as a kite." He spread his arms out. "Bet you I can fly."

Arla pushed his arms down firmly. "Stop it, right now. You're lucky to be alive, Harry."

He gazed at her, and noted the anxiety in her eyes. She wouldn't say it, but he could tell her heart was in turmoil. She was no stranger to violent situations, but this had shaken her badly. He thought of the fierceness in her face when she confronted his attackers. As if she would fly at them with her hands like claws if nothing else. That's what he loved about her. He hooked an arm around her waist and pulled, although that sharpened the pain in the back of his head.

She rested her forehead against his, gently. "I'm sorry," Harry whispered. "I should be saying thank you."

"Yes, you should."

"Thank you, guv."

They kissed lightly and Harry felt her smile against his lips. Then Arla separated.

"This is serious, Harry. Tell me what happened."

"They wanted to know about Rachel – what we've dug up so far. Brian's compromised, which is hard to believe. He was under witness protection." Harry winced as he tried to sit up straighter, and Arla helped him.

"Who could get Brian's new identity?" Arla asked. She answered her own rhetorical question.

"Someone leaked it. We have a mole."

"We do," Harry sighed. "I think Boland and Dempsey were in McPherson's pay, back in the day. And McPherson had something to do with Rachel's murder."

Harry closed his eyes and leaned his head back. The curtains parted and a white coated doctor came in to check on Harry. Arla moved to one side, but her eyes remained on her husband's pale, stricken face. Rage flowed thick and hot in her blood. She would find out who was responsible for this. And she wouldn't rest till she had her revenge.

The doctor turned to Arla. "This could've been a lot worse. The Xrays are normal. I don't think we need a

CT scan of his brain. But if he gets vomiting or drowsiness over the next three days he will need an urgent scan."

"I feel drowsy now, Doc," Harry chirped. "I do like these meds."

"That'll be the morphine, which will wear off in four to six hours. Then you'll feel the pain more. Carry on taking the painkillers for the next few days, and take a break from work."

"I guess I have to ask the boss," Harry grinned at Arla.

"Granted," Arla said. "Now let's take you back home."

***

It was the next morning, and Arla had a meeting with her boss. Commander Wayne Johnson, Deputy Assistant Commissioner of the London Met, paced behind his desk, hands folded behind his back.

Arla, Harry, Lisa, Rob, Ros and Gita sat silently opposite his desk. Arla watched Johnson with trepidation. She knew he wanted to protect his own career, and the name of the police force, before finding justice for his victims. Most of the top brass were like that, despite what they said in public. Her fear now was that Johnson would assign another SIO to the case, someone to keep an eye on Arla, which would be a disaster.

Johnson stopped pacing. He was a bear of a man, rising to more than six feet five and just as wide. But he had small, beady green eyes, and he turned towards them like a pair of LED lights.

"Have you put Boland under surveillance?"

"Not yet sir," Arla said. "But I'd like to."

"Do it now. Tap his phones. Monitor his emails. Yes, I give you permission to start cyber surveillance on him." Johnson waved a large hand dismissively.

"If he knew about McPherson being involved in Rachel Mathews murder, but did nothing, then that's a big red flag. But do we have any evidence of that fact?"

Arla asked, "About McPherson being involved, or about Boland and Dempsey's negligence?"

"Both, damn it," Johnson growled.

"The biggest evidence about McPherson's involvement comes from the way Harry was attacked in Slough," Arla said. "His goons wouldn't have done that without good reason. McPherson knew he was showing his hand. Yet, his aim was to eliminate Harry from the investigation. Maybe he thought Brian had already spoken to Harry, and the game was up."

Johnson looked out the window, his back to them. Then he nodded, turning around. "Yes, that makes sense. But it still won't count as evidence in a court of law, and you know it. Their bloody lawyer will say they wanted Harry for some other reason."

Harry spoke up. "I've never been involved with the McPherson's, sir. However, they might have a link with the Fagan boys. I've heard his name before."

"That's something," Johnson rubbed his smooth chin. Flies would slip on his cheeks, Arla thought.

She said, "And we know Boland didn't follow up on evidence. The CCTV of Simon Barnaby, the Porsche which dropped Rachel off at night, these are vital clues. But that doesn't prove their negligence."

"Have you got the Porsche on CCTV?" Johnson asked.

Rob answered. "Traffic is still looking. They have uncovered a lot but the Porsche remains elusive. Matter of time, hopefully."

"What about Brian Copeland, the informer?"

Harry answered. "He's not responding and not gone back home. He's in hiding, sir. It's possible he knows what happened to Rachel. Or he knows something important."

Johnson put his bear like paws on the back of his armchair, tilting it backward. "When you spoke to Brian, did you mention Boland's name?"

"Yes, I did," Harry said. "On retrospect, that was a mistake. I also mentioned McPherson. I thought the fact he had an identity change would protect him. I didn't think he would be so closely connected to the case."

Johnson waved a hand as if he was swatting a fly. "No time for regrets. You weren't to know."

That surprised Arla. Johnson was normally harsh on his juniors. Was the worm turning? Or perhaps Harry's still visible head injury, encased in the white dressing, caused a change of heart?

"So, what do we know about McPherson?" Johnson asked.

Arla replied. "Scottish immigrant to County Cork in Ireland, where he set up shop with Irish gangsters. He got done for a murder charge, but the witness was murdered. He escaped and settled in London's north west corner, in Islington, where he became friends with some of his Irish gangster friends."

Johnson nodded. "The Cricklewood Crime Syndicate, by any chance? They were UK's biggest OCN at the time."

"The very same. Although McPherson was Scottish, his mother was Irish, and he's a devout Catholic apparently, and still goes to church on Sundays. He became an enforcer for the Cricklewood OCN, and rose rapidly up the ranks. How he's not been convicted as yet, I don't know."

"Where is he now?"

"In Malaga, Spain. He's lived there for the last decade. He's meant to have Irish nationality as well. He still visits London, but not sure where, or when."

Johnson was thoughtful. "And the discovery of Rachel's body was important enough for him to track you guys."

Arla said, "I think sir, that Boland tipped him off. I strongly suspect Boland was in his pay back in the day, as well. Perhaps it was a mistake for me to see Boland."

Arla looked at her feet. Part of her would never forgive herself for what happened to Harry. She couldn't help but blame herself.

Harry spoke slowly, for everyone, but his words were directed at Arla. "If McPherson is involved in Rachel's murder, he would've been interested sooner or later. It's not your fault."

Arla sighed. "I guess what's done is done."

"And what happened actually helped expedite things. Now we know McPherson is involved." Harry's face was like a storm.

Lisa spoke up. "So what are we going to do about McPherson? We can't arrest him. Can we start surveillance? We know he's in London now, spending some time in Islington."

"Yes, start the surveillance," Johnson said. "We need to know every move he makes. Who he calls, who he sees." He frowned and pointed a finger at Arla. "Your report mentioned another man that Rachel was seeing. Simon something?"

"Yes, Simon Barnaby. We know that he exists, but we haven't found him yet." She glanced at the team. "Have we spoken to him?"

Rob answered. "I can't get hold of him. We have his address from the DVLA, but he might have moved home. He wouldn't have gone far, hopefully. I'll do a search on the electoral rolls today."

"We need to find him," Arla said, "But our priority now is McPherson. And we have to lean on Boland, to get more out of him."

Johnson said, "To start the surveillance, you have to liaise with Special Branch." Arla went to protest, but he raised a hand. "No ifs or buts. I want Special Branch in on this. That's better than the MI5, who were involved in the surveillance of the Cricklewood Syndicate."

Arla fumed in silence. She hated the thought of outsiders demanding her cooperation, but she had to admit it was better than the Secret Service, or MI5. They would completely take over the investigation, and she would be left on the sidelines, watching helplessly.

"As you wish, sir," Arla sighed.

"Now go get that bastard McPherson," Johnson growled.

CHAPTER 23

Cora Underwood stood in front of the floor to ceiling glass window of her penthouse apartment on the twentieth floor. She could see London's skyline in the distance, and the city sprawled out beneath. The clouds were still present, and shafts of sunlight broke through, lighting up patches of the East End, and the towers of Canary Wharf.

She had seen the news yesterday. A skeleton found in Regent's Canal. It didn't strike her as important till she got the call. It was her cousin, Richard McPherson. Her mother's brother's son. The other side of the family, the side Cora steered clear of.

They didn't speak often, and when they did, it was a on a burner phone. Cora always kept a couple of them handy. It had been a while since she heard from Richard. He lived in Malaga most of the year.

When he told her, she couldn't believe it. "Are you sure?"

"Unfortunately, yes. My man just informed me. The cops came to see him. He hushed things up back then. The problem went away. But now it seems the cops won't let it go."

“What cops, exactly?”

“A DCI called Arla Baker. She’s the senior investigating officer. She’s got the bit between her teeth about this, for some reason. I asked around, about her. She’s got quite the record. Remember the kiddy fiddlers circle in Westminster? Those old, bent politicians?”

A memory triggered in Cora’s mind. She remembered the scandal of the paedophile gang, whose power and influence had kept them protected for decades.

“Yes, I do. So she was the SIO in that case? That’s just bloody great.”

“I know. But hopefully the problem will go away. I’ll take care of it. I’m calling to give you a heads up. I know your by election is coming up.”

“Thanks. It’s quite tight this time. Labour’s hard on our backs. And the blues brothers aren’t far behind.”

“Blues brothers – the Lib Dems?” Lib Dems stood for the Liberal Democrats, the third largest political party in UK.

“Yes, them.” Cora said. “I can’t let this blow up, Richard. We need to keep it under wraps.”

“There’s nothing to connect to you, so I wouldn’t worry. If anything, they’ll come after me. Let them. They don’t have anything to connect me to the case.”

“Are you sure about that?”

Richard was quiet for a while. “It was a long time ago, so its hard for me to remember. But I don’t think so. In any case, if it comes back to me, I can deal with it.”

Cora paused. “What happened to that girl?”

“I think you know, don’t you?”

Cora was silent for a few seconds. “Thanks for letting me know.”

The conversation now came back to her, as she stood watching the expanse of the city.

To her right, across the Thames, she could see the golden spires of the Houses of Parliament. Some of its windows winked in the sunlight. Soon, she would be in the massive block opposite – where all the MPs (Members of Parliament) had their London offices.

Cora hoped this case would have no connections to her family. Her memory of it was vague, and she didn’t really know anything till one of Rachel’s friends had informed her…what was her name again?

Cora went to her desk, and got busy with answering emails. As the Conservative MP for the borough of Islington, in North West London, she had to meet her constituents daily. This afternoon, she had a surgery planned in a local church, and her diary was already looking full. Naomi, her secretary, called her, and she went through her appointments for the day.

“Don’t forget the meeting with John Deakins.”

“I haven’t. That’s lunchtime, correct?” John Deakins was an old school, white haired Tory MP, and head of the Health Select Committee in Parliament. Health was always a big department, and John had powerful contacts. Cora was working on him, gaining his confidence with her pro market reforms for healthcare.

“Yes. I’ll see you at the office in about half an hour.”

Cora hung up, and went to her bedroom. She lived alone when she was in London, the family home was in Reigate, Surrey. The mansion was on an acre of farm land, and her husband was there now. Their two daughters had grown up and left home for university. Cora checked her personal phone, but she didn’t have any messages from her husband or the girls.

She was getting ready to leave, when her work phone buzzed. It was Naomi, so she answered.

“I’ve got a woman called Melissa Carrington on the phone. She’s a KC Barrister. Says she needs to speak about something important.”

Cora frowned, and searched for the name in the hidden crevices of her mind. Then suddenly, like a jolt in her spine, the name triggered a memory. Melissa – Rachel’s friend. Melissa, who had called her…

Cora sat down at her desk. “Put her through on my other line. Wait. I’ll give you the number.” She gave

Naomi the number of her burner phone, and waited till the phone rang.

“Hi, is that Cora?”

“Melissa?”

“Yes, its me. Thanks for taking my call. How are you?”

They exchanged some pleasantries, but Cora’s heart was thumping. She could guess what this call was about.

“Have you heard about the body they found in Regent’s Canal?” Melissa asked tentatively.

“Yes. And I know it’s Rachel Mathews.”

“Oh?” Melissa was surprised. “Did the police see you as well?”

The first spasm of fear slapped against Cora’s heart, and her heart rate surged. She opened her mouth as she breathed faster. She was glad now she was taking the call on her burner phone.

“No,” Cora said shortly. “When did the police see you?”

“Yesterday afternoon. They asked me about Rachel’s last days, when I saw her, what she was like, and so on.”

“What were the police officer’s names?”

There was a pause as Melissa looked. “Detective Sergeant Rob Pickering and Ros May.”

Cora wrote the names down. “Did they ask you about me? Or…”

“No. But they know about Julia and Kate. Julia reported Rachel as missing as well. The police have spoken to Julia.”

“Did Julia mention me?”

“Not that I know of. I spoke to her after. I believe she’s spoken to Kate as well. I haven’t spoken to Kate. The police will speak to Kate today.”

“Do you have Kate’s number?”

“No. But Julia does.”

“Ok, please send me Julia’s number. I need to speak to her. I don’t want my name associated with this.”

“None of us do,” Melissa said. There was a touch of hardness in her voice. Cora realised she might’ve come across as a touch arrogant. She softened her tone.

“Thank you for letting me know. I know this must be distressing. For all of us.”

“Yes, it is.” They were silent for a while. Cora wondered why Melissa had called her. For reassurance, she thought. Another idea raised its ugly head. But Melissa had as much to lose from this as she did. No, that didn't make sense. Cora could destroy Melissa for this too.

Or could she?

Cora knew she was skating on thin ice. And all because of…

Cora said, "I will make enquiries in the police force. Discreetly, of course."

"Thanks. I hope this blows away soon."

"It will. I've got to go. Please send me Julia's number. I'd like to speak to her and Kate. And Melissa? Please don't call on my regular number. Use this number I'm calling you from now."

"Got it."

CHAPTER 24

The team had gathered in Arla's room. Parmentier, the head of scene of crime was also there. Arla pointed at him to start his report. Parmentier nodded, took a sip of his coffee, and put the mug down on the floor.

"According to the forensics report from 1998, a search of Rachel Mathew's flat had shown her own DNA from her clothes, underwear, toothbrush and shaver. Skin cells were also found on the floor, which matched the DNA of her two friends – Julia Slater and Kate Turner." Parmentier looked up to Arla.

"I think you're in touch with these two women?"

"Yes. Any other DNA samples? From a man?"

Parmentier said, "There's a third woman's sample, as yet unknown. There is a male profile in there as well, according to the historic reports. Both of those DNA samples are unmatched. There was no match in the criminal databases then, and there's no match now. Her friends and contact were all tested back then, including her mother."

Arla tapped an unpainted nail on the table top. "Who signed the report?"

"A Sebastian Collier, Chief Forensic Officer."

So Dempsey or Boland couldn't have stopped the report, Arla thought. The scene of crime officers did their job and filed the report. Hence the two extra DNA profiles, as yet unmatched.

Who could they belong to?

Lisa said, "But guv, in the SIO – Dempsey's – report, these two extra DNA profiles are not mentioned. Is it because they didn't get a match?"

Arla shook her head. "No. They should've mentioned it. From 1984, DNA profiling had started, and by the Nineties, it was widespread. The SIO and his DS, Boland, didn't follow up a lot of leads. Was the male DNA profile checked against her ex-boyfriend – Terry Smith?"

"He had already left for Australia," Rob spoke up. "But when contacted, he agreed to attend a police station in Sydney, and submit a saliva swab. That showed a negative match, so it wasn't Terry. But, we found the elusive Simon Barnaby." Rob paused for effect, and from the tightness in his lips, Arla knew this was important.

"What is it?"

"He's in HMP Pentonville."

A little murmur rippled across the room. Arla said, “I thought he didn’t have a police record?”

“He did, as a juvenile. Until his teenage years, he was caught several times as a messenger for crime syndicates. He carried guns and narcotics for them, and stored them in his parents’ house. But he changed his name when he was eighteen. As soon as he reached mature legal age.”

Arla’s mind was running loops. She scanned the faces of her team, and she knew they were also joining the dots. Rob had probably already done the research, knowing him.

“Go on,” Arla said to Rob.

“He worked for a few OCN’s, back in the day. The Cricklewood Gang was his main employer. When he was caught, he never revealed any names, and as he was under eighteen, he was always released after a short sentences. He claimed innocence – he didn’t know what was in the bags he carried.”

“He was a clean skin,” Lisa said. “Hence the gangs used him, till he wasn’t of use any more.”

“That’s right,” Rob said. “There’s a chance that he came into contact with McPherson. It’s almost certain, in fact. McPherson’s fingerprints were found in a letter inside a bag that Barnaby carried.”

Ros said, “That’s why Barnaby disappeared from London for a while. He came back later with his name change, and new identity.”

Arla raised a hand, and went to the whiteboard. She wrote down the names of Barnaby, McPherson and Rachel.

“What’s the connection here? Rachel was seeing Barnaby before she disappeared. How did she meet him?”

Everyone shrugged. Arla drew an arrow from Rachel to Barnaby and put a question mark next to it.

“And why was this not followed up by Dempsey or Boland? I guess they didn’t check the CCTV to find Simon. Which is negligent in itself, but even if they found him, they might’ve ignored him due to his connection with McPherson.” Arla pointed a finger at Rob. “Good work. Have we got his DNA profile?”

“I’m going to see him today. I spoke to the governor of HMP Pentonville. They’re waiting.”

“Barnaby is now a key suspect. We need to find everything he knows.”

Arla continued. “We also need McPherson’s DNA profile.”

Parmentier said, “I checked on that this morning, after I heard what happened to Harry. I sent the profile to the lab, and waiting to hear back. McPherson has his

DNA and fingerprints when he was arrested once, but then released. We should get the results back today."

Gita spoke up. "There was an unknown woman who visited Rachel's flat, remember? The neighbours saw her, but her three friends – Julia, Melissa and Kate – denied knowing her. The SIO concluded the neighbours might be mistaken, but the female DNA profile wasn't chased up."

"So we have an unknown man and woman who visited Rachel's flat. We need to find them, people. Let's hurry up."

Arla stood and paced the little space behind her desk. The room was cramped with everyone sitting opposite her. She missed Harry, who would now be standing against the doorframe, listening intently. He had been ordered to rest for the day, and she was glad.

"The DI from Special Branch will be here soon," Arla said. "I'll bring him up to speed, and then we pay Mr McPherson a visit. Apparently, McPherson is in London, travelling with his Spanish passport."

Gita said, "Ros and I are going to see Kate Turner. Hopefully she can cast some new light on the case."

Rob looked at Ros, a little forlorn. Arla noted the look. Rob and Ros were still dating, as far as she knew. She didn't know the latest gossip, but it seemed Rob was still holding a light for Ros. But she wasn't sure if Ros was feeling the same.

"Alright," Arla nodded. "I'll contact Dr Banerjee to see if he has an update from Prof Robinson, the forensic anthropologist. Let's meet back here later for a catch up."

***

The team dispersed, and Arla went to the front desk, where the DI from Special Branch was waiting. He was sitting opposite the desk, a briefcase clutched in his hand. He rose as Arla approached. A handsome man, Arla noted, with flecks of white in his hair, which matched the salt and pepper, well-trimmed beard. He was about six feet tall, with large, attentive hazel eyes that focused on her. A dark blue suit hugged his lean, athletic frame.

Arla extended a hand. "DI Greg Warren?"

"You must be the famous Arla Baker," Greg smiled, his white teeth flashing. They shook hands.

Arla led them back through the double doors, and then into the corridor of the station. Arla offered him tea or coffee, and they stopped at the canteen on the way to her office.

Arla guessed Greg was in his fifties. His lean, tanned face looked healthy, but with the lines of his age around the corners of his eyes, and on his forehead. She knew he was an experienced officer who had worked in special situations – surveillance, investigating foreigners and dangerous criminals, or politicians – for many years.

"What do think of the case so far?" Arla asked, as she paid for two coffees, and handed one to Greg.

"Cold cases are always difficult, aren't they? But the forensics are your best bet, I guess."

"Yes." Arla told him about the DNA profiles, and Gregg nodded.

"You wont have much CCTV from that time, which is a shame. But your report said you found a man that the victim was seeing just before she died? He must be your main suspect now."

"He is, and we're seeing him today. He's not running away, which is a good sign. But McPherson is also our main suspect now. He's clearly got something to hide."

They had reached Arla's office, and Greg sat down opposite the desk. "Yes, he does. Hence the heavy-handed response to the informer being questioned. Have you found the informer, by the way?"

"Brian Copeland? Not yet. I'm worried about him. If they came after Harry, what would they do to him?"

"He might be in hiding. If he was in the witness protection programme, he could call the secure line for help." Greg looked down at his phone. "His real name is Garth Davies. But his car and home is in his new name. Have you tried to track his movements on CCTV?"

“Yes. His car is still at the house. We’re not sure where he went after he left the house yesterday. CCTV hasn’t picked him up yet. But I know Traffic are looking at Slough train and bus stations to see if they can catch him.”

Greg nodded. “We need to find him.”

“So, when do we pay Mr McPherson a visit?”

Greg exhaled and settled back into his chair. “He’s as slippery as an eel. As you know, he’s been arrested several times in his long life. He’s in his sixties now, and Interpol suspect him to be active in at least two crime syndicates operating from southern Spain. Suspect, but not definite. He’s very careful not to show his face anywhere. He just happened to be in London when Rachel’s body was discovered.”

“Why does he come to London?”

“Well, he’s got legitimate business interests all over the country. And believe it or not, despite his crimes, it is impossible to pin anything on him. His lawyers have sharp teeth. They question every taped phone call, every criminal who mentions his name.” Greg spread his hands, and his jaws tightened in frustration. “Men like him are hard to pin down.”

“But he’s slipped up now, hasn’t he?”

“Has he? I’m sorry for what happened to your partner – but it’s his word against the lawyer’s when he says he heard McPherson's name from his attackers. That's not proof, and you know that."

"Yes, I do," Arla said, her eyes flashing. "But we need to do something. Both of us know McPherson is involved in this, and to be honest, I think he's running scared. There's something big at play here."

Greg nodded slowly. "What do you think that might be?"

"I don't know as yet. Were Boland and Dempsey in McPherson's pay?"

"We have suspected that for many years, yes. Not just them, but other officers as well. The Cricklewood Crime Syndicate, where McPherson rose up the ranks to become the top man, had a few police officers in their payroll."

"Do you have any proof?"

Greg shook his head slowly, and he pressed his lips downward. "Unfortunately, no. The ACU investigated Boland and Dempsey, didn't they?"

"Yes, they didn't find anything." Arla frowned. "But Boland effectively told me to back off. I wonder why he did that."

"He showed his hand as well," Greg reflected. "I think he's also worried."

"I want to speak to McPherson," Arla said, decisively. She leaned forward and stared at Greg. "Can you make that happen?"

CHAPTER 25

HMP Pentonville was a Category B prison. That meant it was not used to keep serial killers and ultra-violent offenders, but more the ordinary criminals like OCN members, armed robbers and burglars. More visitors were allowed, and inmates were given more privileges like mixing in the recreation grounds.

Rob and Lisa walked from Bransbury Station, a smaller district near Islington, and walked down Caledonian Road towards the prison.

Lisa saw that Rob was tight lipped, and quieter than he usually was. "You alright?" she asked. Lisa had worked with Rob for many years, and she knew him inside out.

"Yes, I'm all good." Rob scratched his beard but declined from further comment.

Lisa watched him. Rob had lost a lot of weight in the last year or so, and he looked svelte and trim. But he didn't look happy.

"How's things between you and Ros?" Lisa asked. "You can tell me to piss off, I don't mind. None of my business, after all."

Rob sighed, and didn't say anything for a while. They walked in silence. The white towers of HMP Pentonville were visible in the mid distance.

"She's not sure if its going to work out. She doesn't want to start a family now."

Lisa knew there was about eight years age gap, with Rob being older. He was in his late thirties now.

"You want to have children?" Lisa asked.

Rob shrugged. "Yes. I mean, I'm not getting any younger. There will come a time in my life when I'll wonder what it would've been like to be a dad. By then, it might be too late."

"Not necessarily. Men don't have a biological clock. It depends on the woman."

Rob smiled, but it was forced. "My dad was fifty-five when I was born. Seventy when I was fifteen. He couldn't do a lot of things that my friends dads did. He stayed in his room when we went on holidays. Didn't come to watch me play football as he was sick. He died when I was twenty."

"I'm sorry," Lisa said. She squeezed Rob's arm. "I didn't know that about your dad."

She could see the dilemma now. Rob liked Ros a lot, maybe even loved her, but she wanted to wait for a few years before having children. Lisa couldn't blame Ros for that, either. Ros wanted to have career, and she had worked hard for it. And she still had time, four or five years at least before she had children.

"Give it some time," Lisa said. "Both of you have time."

Rob shook his head. "I'm not sure if I do. I don't want to be an old man with a young child."

"You won't be. Charlene was forty when we adopted Jack. He's ten now, and it's fine." Lisa was in a same sex relationship with her long-term partner, and they had a boy.

Rob smiled. "Must be fun at home."

"It can be crazy, I must admit," Lisa laughed. "I got back home the other evening and Jack was literally climbing the wall – he wanted to see if he could reach the top shelf of the book case. Charlene was in the kitchen, she heard my scream and came running. She's taller than me, so she got Jack down safely."

They got to the prison gates, and showed their warrant cards. The guard called inside, and then waved them through. Lisa noted the broken windows on the high walls of the inner sanctum, as she walked through the massive gates. HMP Pentonville had a number of break outs over the years. Recently, security had been bolstered.

They were led through the wide corridors, and asked to wait inside an office while the prison guards went to get Simon Barnaby. He had agreed to see them without a lawyer.

Rob laid out Barnaby's file on the desk. "He was caught with guns and cash in his car. They were hidden under the driver's seat in a special compartment."

"So he reverted to his previous life," Lisa said. "When did this happen?"

"Last year. He's got a sentence for eight years, out in six with good behaviour."

"He's sixty years old now," Lisa pointed to his DOB. "He was thirty-two when he was seen with Rachel. He'll be sixty-six when he's out. Not nice, being in jail at this age, eh?"

Their conversation was cut short by the guards entering. Simon Barnaby was handcuffed. The guard put him in the chair opposite the desk where Lisa and Rob sat. Then they took the handcuffs off.

Barnaby was staring at them. Lisa saw an old man with hair only at the sides, wrinkles deep in his forehead and cheeks sagging with time. There was a dull, cold look in his dark, lifeless eyes. Lisa saw no emotion in his face, just a blank nothingness.

"Do you want us to stay here?" One of the guards asked.

Rob shook his head. “No, leave us alone.”

“He’s been searched head to toe. Nothing on him,” the guard said. “Press the buzzer under the desk if he tries anything.”

“We will,” Rob said. He noted Barnaby’s still stocky, stout shoulders. He wore a long sleeved shirt, but the forearms filled out the sleeves. His muscles had gone to fat with age, but this man had been strong once. There was an implacable look on his face, as if nothing scared or worried him anymore. Rob had seen ex-cons like him before. Men who feared nothing because they had seen the worst. But he also sensed a vulnerability in the man. And Rob knew why.

He introduced Lisa and himself.

“Twenty-eight years ago you knew a woman called Rachel Mathews. She lived in Angel. Do you remember?”

A light appeared in the scales of Barnaby’s eyes, then sharpened focus. The corners of his eyes crinkled, deepening the lines.

“Is that what you came here for?” Barnaby spoke in a hoarse voice that spoke of a lifelong smoking habit. Rob kept his focus on him.

“Rachel disappeared twenty-eight years ago on 22nd October 1998. She was seen with you on 18th October, 15th, 12th and 10th. You also saw her twice in late September. Each time you were seen with her on CCTV."

Lisa slid forward the tablet device, but kept it in her hands. On the screen, the black and white image showed Rachel and Barnaby walking, holding hands. She swiped left, and showed him the other images.

"That's you, Simon Barnaby, twenty-eight years ago," Rob said. "Correct?"

Barnaby's jaws were clamped tight, and his nostrils flared. The light had faded in his eyes, and the snake like stare was back.

"What do you want?"

"We want to know what happened to Rachel."

"Why?"

"We found her body in Regent's Canal. It was wrapped inside a tarpaulin and tied with stones to make it sink. DNA and dental records prove it was Rachel Mathews."

Barnaby's eyes widened, and his jaws ground together as he listened.

Rob said, "We believe Rachel was killed. Did you do it?"

Patches of colour had appeared on Barnaby's pale face. His lips tightened, and a single word emerged like a quiet snarl. "No."

"Where were you from 20th till 22nd October, 1998?"

"I was in London. Working as a garage mechanic. I didn't see Rachel during the days you mentioned."

Lisa cleared her throat. "Tell us how you met her."

Barnaby turned to her, his expression that of a boxer weighing up his opponent. He appeared to soften a little. "In the pub."

Rob didn't believe him, and from the way Lisa snorted, it was clear what she thought. Lisa said, "We could do this all day, Mr Barnaby, and not get anywhere. Why don't you tell us the truth? How did you meet Rachel?"

"I told you. In the pub. It was in Angel. The Anglesey Arms or something like that. Not sure if it still exists."

"What did Rachel know about Mr Ian McPherson?"

The sudden change threw Barnaby off guard. He frowned, which deepened and rippled across his face like a chainsaw running through a painting.

"I don't know what you're talking about."

"Mr McPherson knew Rachel as well, didn't he? Is that how you met Rachel? Through your boss?"

The scowl on Barnaby's face wasn't just anger, it was also confusion. Lisa stared back at him, but the older man blinked, and sat back in his chair.

"I don't know what the hell you're here for. Yes, I did go out with Rachel for a while. A few weeks. It wasn't long. Then we split up and I never saw her again."

Lisa flicked her eyes at Rob. Barnaby had confessed to knowing Rachel. Granted, he had no choice given the CCTV evidence. But would he have been so open about it if he had killed her?

Rob nodded at Lisa, and she continued. "We have evidence that shows McPherson knew Rachel. Can you tell us about their relationship?"

It was a half-truth as they didn't have concrete evidence. But Harry almost got killed for chasing up McPherson. That was proof enough for them.

"I don't know anything about that." He shook his head, and put his palms on the table. "Will that be all?"

Rob asked, "Why did you agree to see us without a lawyer?"

The palms slipped from the table. Barnaby glared at Rob, the black eyes glinting. His previous flatness was now ruffled, and he didn't care.

"I thought you would be sensible. You came here to talk about something useful."

"Like cutting a deal with you?"

Barnaby made a growling sound in his throat, and then he rose. As he reached for the door handle, Lisa said, “Emily Peabody. Lives in Amersham. She’s your daughter, isn’t she? Changed her last name after marriage.”

Barnaby stopped, his hand still on the handle. He had his back to them, and didn’t move. Lisa continued.

“We spoke to Emily this morning. She’s six months pregnant. You’ll be a grandfather soon, but you won’t see your grandchild for many years.”

Barnaby took his hand off the door handle. He looked to the ceiling and exhaled.

Lisa and Rob glanced at each other. Rob said, “Why don’t you tell us about the connection between Rachel and McPherson.

Barnaby turned slowly. He didn’t move from where he was. “You think it’s that easy? I have a family to protect. You have no idea.”

“We do. We can offer you-

“It’s not going to work!” Barnaby shouted suddenly, his face flushing crimson. A vein bulged and throbbed on his forehead. He put a hand to his forehead and swore softly. Then he staggered back to the chair and sat down wearily.

Rob knew Barnaby was scared. Criminals gained a lot of respect if they didn’t give away their bosses, if they didn’t cut a deal with the police for a shorter sentence. And if they didn't – they could be dead in a ditch when they were free. Like Brian Copeland, who was still in hiding.

"If you don't want to mention McPherson that's fine. But give us something."

Barnaby raised his head slowly. He gazed at Rob without blinking. Then a shadow passed over his face, like a veil was being slowly removed. The broken shell of a man emerged, a man bare as a tree in dead winter.

"Rachel was with another man. She didn't like him. But he had this hold on her. He controlled her. She wanted to be free from him. But she couldn't."

Lisa frowned. "Who was he?"

Barnaby looked at her. Lisa had a sinking feeling when she saw the sudden fear in the old man's eyes. He shivered once, as if the room was suddenly cold.

"I don't know. But he was…bad to her."

"In what way?"

"She had marks on her back, like someone had put needles into her skin. Not scratch marks, or whiplashes. But neat holes, where the skin was punctured." Barnaby stopped, and stared into the distance. Then he passed a hand over his face.

"What were the puncture marks for?" Lisa asked, a coldness seeping into her limbs.

"To hang her up by hooks," Barnaby said, a rictus of fear now contorting his face. "He did it when she was drowsy with drugs he mixed in her drinks. He got a kick out of torturing her."

"Who was he?" Rob repeated. "Was it McPherson?"

Barnaby's eyes remained on Rob, then they slowly slid down to the floor. He shook his head, once, without looking at them.

"No," he replied hoarsely.

"Then who was it? Give us a name."

"I don't know." The old man stared at them in silence, then down at the carpet.

"I need to go now." Barnaby stood, and turned away.

CHAPTER 26

"That's McPherson's house," Greg pointed from inside the car. Arla was sat next to him. They were in Cricklewood, a stone's throw from Islington, but it seemed like a world apart. The shop windows were either boarded up, or marked with graffiti. Pound shops and pawnbrokers huddled close together in that grimy, gritty streetscape of inner city London. Narrow, tall terraced houses stood miserably, paint peeling, and some of their residents sitting on the steps.

Greg had turned into a side street, and it was quieter here, the rush of the many hued pedestrians on the main avenue absent. They were parked behind a van, and Arla couldn't see the house that Greg was pointing at. She knew he had parked behind the van so they wouldn't be spotted. She looked at the streetlight at the beginning and the end of the street.

"No CCTV camera's," she remarked. "What door number is it?"

"Thirty one. We only now because we intercepted one of his men arriving there. By intercepted, I mean digitally. We tracked his phone's location by triangulation. There might not be cameras here, but there's plenty of phone masts to get the phone signal from."

Arla nodded. She was glad Greg had joined the investigation. She had a strong impulse to get out of the car, march to number thirty one and demand to see McPherson. But that would be the wrong move.

Greg said, "A new car parked on this street would be noticed. I'm sure McPherson's men watch the cars."

A couple of men walked past, dressed in jeans and light jackets. It was cloudy still, but warm. They cast a casual look at the car.

"You're right. I wanted to see if we could get a glimpse of him. But perhaps this was the wrong idea."

Arla seethed inside. She wanted to do something, get revenge for what happened to Harry. If he was here, he'd be telling her she was being her emotional and impulsive self. And he would be right. Too many times, Arla wore her heart on her sleeve, and ended up in trouble.

"Not necessarily," Greg commented. "If anyone visits him, we might be able to see that person. But let's ask the surveillance team. They're also parked close by, and one of them is a beggar on the street corner. On your side of the street. Can you see him?"

Arla put her window down, and tilted her head a fraction, without leaning her head out of the window. She could see the man sitting on a rug, with a dog beside him. He was patting the dog's head. He had two brown paper placards next to him, but Arla couldn't read the print. Probably lamenting the cause of his homelessness.

"He's got a cute dog," she grinned.

"It's a sniffer dog. Just in case we have to bust into a house to search for stuff, or hidden human beings."

Arla nodded. "Some of these terraced houses connect with each other, don't they?"

"Yes. I wouldn't be surprised if the OCN owned or rented several houses in this street."

Greg's radio beeped and he answered. A voice crackled on the speaker. "DC Perkins speaking. IC1 male approaching the house. Standing by."

"Do you recognise him?" Greg asked.

"Negative, but facial recognition in progress. Will update you asap."

Arla couldn't see the man from her side of the car. Greg couldn't either, and they couldn't get out to look.

"I guess we just have to wait," Arla said, her nails digging into her palm. The seconds ticked by, increasing Arla's frustration. Then the radio crackled again.

"We have a match. The person is Brian Copeland. Repeat, Brian Copeland."

Arla spoke rapidly. "The man we went to question in Slough? The one under witness protection?"

"Positive."

Patterns were forming rapidly in Arla's mind, spreading like the lines on a map. Brian knew something important, otherwise he wouldn't have run. Harry had told him he wanted to know if McPherson had a connection to Rachel Mathews. When Brian heard the news, he made a run for it.

Arla had assumed Brian was hunted, but now she knew different. Brian had leaked the news to McPherson. Hence they were ready when Arla and Harry arrived in Slough.

That was also the reason Brian was here now. He was still in McPherson's pay, despite being an informer for the police. Brian was playing both sides. But there was something more important. Brian knew about the critical connection between McPherson and Rachel – hence he went on the run, after informing his boss the police wanted to speak to him.

Ergo – they needed to catch Brian.

Sparks of electricity showered in her brain, and she turned to Greg. "We need to get Brian. Now!" She tried to get out of the car, but Greg pulled her back.

"If you get out now you give the game away. Leave him be for the time being. Lets see what he does."

Arla shook her head. "Brian's the missing link. Later might be too late. I need to speak to him."

Greg pulled harder on her elbow. "Just wait. Let me ask one of the surveillance team to approach him. It's better that way."

Arla wasn't happy, but she agreed. "Make sure they stop him."

Greg spoke rapidly on his radio. "Approach Brian Copelan. Repeat, approach him. Inform him we need to speak to him."

"Or arrest him," Arla said on the radio. "DCI Baker speaking."

"Roger that."

Arla turned to Greg. "Start driving. I want to see how Brian reacts."

"Are you sure?" Greg was scpetical. "We should let the team handle this."

"We will. We can just drive past."

Greg looked undecided, but eventually followed Arla's direction. He indicated, then pulled out on the street. As they got to the end, they two men in casual clothes approach a man walking from the other direction. The man stopped suddenly. Then he turned and ran. The two men ran after him.

“Damn,” Arla swore. “Speed up.”

Greg pressed his foot down, and the car surged forward. They saw Brian climb up a wall, jump down, disappearing from view. The wall formed the boundary of a park. Greg screeched the car to a stop, and they ran inside the park, hot on the heels of the two plain clothes officers.

The park wasn’t big, and there was a children’s soft play area inside. Arla watched as Brian got to the other end of the park, and jumped on the railings, then vaulted over it. Breath rasped in her lungs as she willed her legs to move faster. Her thighs burned with the effort. She left Greg behind, catching up with the two younger officers as the scaled the railings. One of them helped her to climb over, then she jumped, landing on her feet.

Brian was getting away. Arla chased, sweat now pouring down her face, sticking the shirt to her chest. She watched helplessly as Brian got into a car, and drove off. Traffic was light, and the car was soon fading from view. She screamed in rage and frustration.

Greg had caught up with her. He was panting. "Don't worry," he gasped. "Traffic can get him on CCTV. Let's get back to the nick."

CHAPTER 27

Chris had watched the detectives chase Brian with interest. So, they knew. They had figured out Brian was the missing link. But Brian couldn't be caught. Chris had never trusted the man, and he had only employed Brian because he was advised to do so. Brian didn't have the guts to follow Chris's orders. He didn't understand.

Chris followed the detectives as they ran inside the park. He noticed the woman with dark hair. He had seen her before. Arla Baker. A narrow face, sunken cheeks, glinting eyes. Athletic as well, given the way she ran and vaulted across the park railings. Chris didn't chase after them. He merely watched. He waited. The two things he was good at.

He sauntered to the end of the park, and he was just in time to see Brian drive off. He was too far to see the registration plate of the car, which was a shame. Chris wanted to catch up with Brian. They had a lot to discuss.

He saw the detectives run back to their car, and drive off. He could tell they were frustrated. Arla Baker especially. She was fuming. Her cheeks were red with the running effort, and he thought she looked beautiful. He had a vision of Arla on her knees, hands and feet tied. Looking up at him with a silent plea in her eyes.

His eyes widened as desire jolted in his heart. The detectives drove away, and Chris played the fantasy in his mind. He hadn't indulged in his fantasies for a long time. He was in his fifties now, and his body didn't feel the same way. He walked around north London, visiting the spots where he had kept his victims. He liked to reminisce, but with Rachel's discovery, his peace had been shattered. He liked to think he had retired, but now, the old ghost had returned, and he could feel the warm hand on his shoulder.

Maybe it was time. Could Arla Baker be his next victim? The thought was a tantalising one. It would set the entire police force in a tizzy. But he had to be careful. His ambition could also be his downfall.

He had followed Arla Baker around, ever since he saw her by Regent's Canal. He had seen her leave for Slough. He didn't follow her there, and neither did he know the purpose of their visit. Did they go there to look for Brian? Is that why Brian was here?

Chris thought of Rachel's friends – Julia, Melissa and Kate. He had not spoken to them in years. Perhaps now was the time to make contact again. He didn't have their numbers, but he knew someone who might. He called her.

"I told you not to call this number," the woman's voice was harsh.

"Don't be like that. When was the last time I spoke to you?"

"What do you want?"

"I want to speak to Rachel's friends again. Julia and that lot. Do you have their numbers?"

"No, I don't."

Something in her voice told Chris she was lying. "I think you do. You stayed in touch with them. Especially that Melisssa. You met up with her."

"Chris stop this, right now. Stay away from those women. Do you understand?"

"I just want to talk to them. That's all."

"I said no." The woman paused. "I've got to go."

She hung up on him. Chris stared at the phone, and anger surged through him. How dare she treat him like that? Chris hated others standing in the way of his needs.

And right now, he felt the need to contact one of Rachel's friends.

CHAPTER 28

Gita and Ros got off the train at Broadstairs in Kent, and walked down the hill from the station. The sea lay on their left, unfurling to the horizon. White lines appeared like a series of giant exclamation marks on the blue water, and after a while, Gita realised they were wind farms. She was surprised by the density of the wind turbines. They were far out to sea, and if they went closer by boat, she knew they would be gigantic. She had seen wind farms driving down the motorway, when she went up north to see her parents.

Ros was also staring at them, and narrowly avoided a puddle on the pavement. She turned to Gita.

"I wish clean energy meant our utility bills would fall. Not a chance, eh?"

"Nope."

Broadstairs wasn't a big town, and they were able to walk to Kate Turner's office. She was waiting for them outside. Kate was in her middle ages now, fifty three according to her records. She was still pretty, but a love of sun had left her skin loose on the cheeks, but she had managed to look after herself well. A natural blonde, her hair cascaded past her shoulders.

Gita saw a tiredness in her eyes, similar to what she felt when she looked at herself in the morning. Kate had the look of a woman who didn't like what she saw in the mirror – and it wasn't her appearance.

Ros and Gita introduced themselves. Kate said, "Shall we go to the café around the corner? It's quiet there and no one will bother us."

Gita knew Kate wanted to avoid her inquisitive colleagues, which made sense. They could always speak to Kate's boss later, if required. Kate led them a short walk down the road. Broadstairs was busy in the summer, and families flocked on the sunny street. They turned left, down a quieter street, and went inside a café. Kate went upstairs. There was only one person by the window, and Kate sat down in a corner opposite, where they could talk in privacy.

"It's been such a long time since Rachel disappeared," Kate said. "A lifetime, really."

"Thank you for speaking to us," Ros said. "Tell us about Rachel, please."

"She was a quiet person. But when with her close friends, she opened up. She had suffered with depression, as you must know."

Kate talked further about Rachel, and to both the detectives, it was a repeat of what they had heard from Julia, and Melissa. Gita wondered if the three women had talked. She decided to be open about it.

Kate blinked a couple of times. "No, we haven't. When I moved away from London, I lost touch with them. I prefer it here."

Gita thought Kate's easy attitude was a little forced now. It was in the tightness of her eyelids, a contraction of her neck muscles.

Ros asked, "When did you last see Rachel?"

"About two weeks before the 22nd October. That was the day she was reported missing, right? Julia got in touch with me, and she said she met Sarah, Rachel's mother. I told her to report her missing. I went round to the flat, but as you know, Rachel wasn't there."

Ros nodded in silence. "Rachel's neighbours saw a fourth woman who came to her flat. We know that you three went to her flat. Do you know who the other woman might be?"

Kate down turned her lips and shrugged. "Maybe one of Rachel's friends from work? Sorry, I don't know."

"And there was also a man," Ros said slowly. "Whose DNA was found in the flat. It wasn't her ex-boyfriend, Terry Smith. Do you know who that might be?"

Kate appeared to think for a while. Then she shook her head slowly. "No, sorry."

Ros glanced at Gita, who took over. "Did you and Rachel talk about person stuff?"

"Like all friends do, I guess. Yes, we did."

"This might sound a little odd. Was Rachel into violent sex?"

Kate looked like she'd been slapped. She was stunned into silence. Her lips moved, but she didn't speak, as if her lips had formed the words, but her mind couldn't utter them.

Ros and Gita looked on with interest. Kate swallowed once, and recovered. "Well, it depends what you mean by that. I mean," She paused again, and Ros could see she was weighing up her options. Trying to think ahead. Should she lie? Would it implicate her in anything?

"It's very simple," Gita said softly. "Either Rachel was into violent sex, or she wasn't. What did she tell you?"

Gita kept her attention on Kate. "And please tell us the truth. You're not in any trouble. We need to know what Rachel was like."

Kate exhaled, and the sound was like air escaping from a punctured balloon. The tension dissipated from her shoulders. Her fingers touched her forehead, then lowered slowly to her lap.

"Oh god. Yes. We had this chat once. She told me she liked to be slapped, or hit, before she had sex. The pain turned her on. She couldn't explain it herself, and I didn't understand it. I told her it was weird."

They were silent for a while. Ros looked at Gita, and they both knew this was important. Kate had been evasive until now. She wasn't holding back anymore.

"Did she tell you who she engaged in that with?"

Kate shrugged. "The men she dated. I guess so, anyway."

"She didn't mention anyone specific?"

A shadow passed over Kate again, and Ros saw her previous expression flicker across her face. The same cloud of evasion, that had hovered over Kate, ever since they entered this room. Ros couldn't put her finger on it, but she didn't like it.

"No, she didn't," Kate said.

"Was she ever hurt as a result of this violent sex? I mean, physically."

Kate sighed. "Detective, this is a long time ago. We were young, and we did some stupid things. I don't know if this was a phase that Julia was going through. And no, I don't know if she got physically hurt. She didn't tell me if she did."

Gita said, "But if she was being hit – or assaulted by force, like being kicked or punched, then that would hurt, right?"

Kate turned her neck slowly. She didn't like Gita's tone. Her chin lifted a fraction, and a cold arrogance registered on her face.

"I guess that's obvious."

"But you didn't see a black eye, or any other injuries on her? And you never asked her about getting hurt as a result of this?"

"No, I didn't."

Ros and Gita exchanged a glance. Neither of them believed Kate anymore. But they had prepared for this. Rob and Lisa had updated them about Simon Barnaby's revelations.

Ros said, "We have reason to believe Rachel was in a physically abusive relationship with a man. He hurt Rachel, tortured her, in fact. Do you know anything about that?"

Gita could almost hear Kate's heart booming loudly. Spots of colour appeared on Kate's cheeks. Her lips opened and she breathed faster.

Then she shook her head. "No, I don't, sorry. That…that's awful."

Again, Gita got the feeling Kate was acting. She was trying too hard, and the truth was pressing in the back of her mind like a tornado against a flimsy curtain. Any second now, the thin barrier would collapse, and Kate would be borne away by the dark winds.

Gita said, "You were close to Rachel, right? Closer than she was to Julia, or Melissa?"

Kate blinked. "What makes you say that?"

"Just the impression we got from speaking to the others. My point is – if Rachel opened up to you about her preference for violent sex, would she not disclose the name of the man who was subjecting her to torture? The man she was trying to get free from?"

A cloud hovered above them, dense, humid, thick with tension. Kate stared at Gita, looking like a woman walking a tight rope between two mountain peaks.

Lisa spoke softly. "If you know, Kate, then tell us. Do it for Rachel. We think this man killed her. We need to find him."

Kate slid her eyes to Lisa, and a fractured, broken expression shimmered across her face, like a mirage in the desert. She licked her lips.

"I'm so sorry. I wish I could help you. I don't know."

CHAPTER 29

After the interview with the detectives, Kate had taken sick leave from work. She claimed a headache, which was actually true. Now she was back home, and she paced the floor of her third floor flat. She felt restless. She suspected the police didn't believe her. And if they found out…

She pulled out her phone and called Julia. She didn't answer. Kate couldn't think any more. She felt her skin itching, and bile rising up in her throat. Nausea curdled in her guts. She went to the bathroom, and tried to vomit, but only bile came up. She sank back on the sofa, the headache now raging in her temples, like a caged lion wanting to be released.

She picked up her phone again, and saw she had a missed call from Julia. She called back.

"I can't take this anymore," she said to Julia. "The cops came to see me today. They know what happened."

"What do you mean, they know what happened?"

Kate closed her eyes, and touched her fingertips to her forehead. “I think they know about him.” Kate was too scared to even utter the man’s name. She shuddered. This was the reason she’d left London. She never wanted to see him again.

“How?” Julia’s voice was sharp. “What did you tell them?”

“I told them nothing!” Kate shouted back. “Bloody nothing, like you told me to! This is your fault. Yours and that bitch, Melissa’s. We should have told the police ages ago about what happened. But you didn’t and now look.”

“Calm down.”

“Oh really? This is not going away, Julia. The cops won’t let this go. They’re going to find out.”

“Whatever happens, we need to stick together. I’ve spoken to Melissa, and she’s talked to Cora. We need to show a united front. The police will ask questions – let them. That’s their job. Let them dig around. It’s been almost thirty years, they won’t be able to prove anything.”

“That’s what you think. I’ve got a bad feeling about this.”

Kate paused. Memories surfaced inside her again, visions she kept in the dungeons of her mind. They were crawling out now, reaching sharp nails to rip down the back of her mind, corroding her peace.

"Look, Kate. You can't change the past. But we can do something about what happens now. You just need to play your part. Okay?"

"Play my part? You think this is some bloody game?" Kate scoffed, and ground her teeth together. "You know why I don't stay in touch with you anymore, Julia? You and Melissa were always the same. Your ambition turned into greed, and that's all you cared about. You never cared about Rachel. Or me, or anyone else. It's all about you, isn't it?"

Julia was silent. Kate breathed against the receiver, her mind banging like a drum.

Julia spoke in a whisper. "Just hold it together for a little longer. It's going to be alright."

"That's what you think."

CHAPTER 30

Arla stood behind the Traffic sergeant, and watched the bank of TV screens on his desk. Brian's grey VW was visible, speeding down the road. Another squad car that was patrolling nearby had been called to assist. Greg stood next to her. The VW went down an alley and vanished from view, then reappeared again. But eventually, they lost the car in a maze of streets in Cricklewood's narrow alleys.

"We found the empty car in a disused garage," the traffic sergeant pointed at the screen in the middle. "There was nothing inside. The glove compartment was empty."

"And two uniform units are now searching the houses in a one-mile radius," Arla shook her head. "But they've not found anything as yet. He can't be far, can he?"

Greg said, "Those streets are rough. Lots of council housing, and two big estates. He could be anywhere in that rabbit warren."

"This used to be the stomping ground of the Cricklewood Crime Syndicate," Greg continued, referring to the OCN. "Brian worked for them, so he will know the hiding holes."

"We have informers there too," Arla said, crossing her arms across her chest. "I've spoken to DI Sanderson of the Angel police station. He's going to put out a team of plain clothes constables to ask around the estates. With any luck, we should find him soon."

"We're going to need that luck," Greg said. "I hope he's not got out of the area already. Cricklewood is close to King's Cross station."

"We have his face up on every CCTV in the station. Facial recognition should catch him if he goes into a train or bus stop."

Greg nodded. Arla glanced at him. She should've listened to him instead of trying to stop Brian. Then they might have caught him while he was leaving the house. Greg was a senior officer, and his experience showed.

Arla's radio crackled and she answered. It was DI Sanderson. "One of our team has spoken to a couple of the lads outside the Greyfriars Council Estate – close to where Brian's car was found. We have a match with Brian – a man who went upstairs. We've got the building under lockdown. We'll let you know if we find him."

"Excellent," Arla enthused, a clutch of adrenaline spreading across her tired limbs. "I'll wait to hear from you."

She turned to Greg and told him the news. Greg nodded, and glanced at his watch. It was close to six pm.

"I need to get back to my office. My boss will want a report. Is that okay?"

"Thanks for your help today," Arla said, and meant it. At least, now she knew where McPherson was, although she doubted he would remain there for too long.

"As soon as we get hold of Brian, I'll let you know."

Greg thanked her, and left. Arla stayed in the Traffic control room for a while, watching the screens and chatting with the traffic sergeant. She didn't get another call from DI Sanderson, but she knew the DI would call her as soon as he heard anything.

Down in the open plan office, the team had gathered back. Gita and Ros stood in front of Rob's desk, deep in conversation. She got up to them and said hello.

"Just got back from Kent, guv," Ros said. "Kate Turner's lying through her teeth."

Gita added, "I got the impression she had no choice. She's running scared. The question is why, after all these years."

Ros nodded. "We got the same impression from speaking to Julia Slater, didn't we? She's acting funny. Melissa Carrington was the same."

"There's something going on between them, that's for sure. I think they know who the unknown man and woman are."

"What makes you say that?" Arla asked.

Gita said, "Well, their stories seem well rehearsed, for one thing. All three of them said the same thing. But Kate seemed the closest to cracking to be honest. She was also the only one who came clean about Rachel's fetish for violent sex."

"Did the others know?"

Ros and Gita glanced at each other. "I think so," Ros said, and Gita agreed. "When they denied knowledge, it seemed forced. If Rachel was close to them, then how could they not know? Especially Julia, who reported her missing.

Lisa came back, holding a tray of tea and coffee. The others thanked her and took their drinks. Lisa glanced at Rob.

"Have you told the guv about Barnaby?"

"Yes, I heard," Arla said. She had a quick chat with Rob on the way back from Cricklewood. "Do you think Rachel's friends know who this man is? Or was?"

"How could they not?" Gita said. "They were close friends. I'm positive that Kate knew. If she did, how could the other two not?"

"Any sign of the owner of the Porsche that dropped Rachel off? We find that car, we find something concrete. I'm not saying the driver of the Porsche was the man Rachel was seeing, but its important."

"Traffic are still looking, guv," Rob said, shrugging. "It's not easy, given there's not much in the way of footage, and they can't use ANPR either."

Automatic Number Plate Recognition was not in force in 1998, Arla knew that. "Tell them to keep looking. I'll update with them."

Arla noted the uncomfortable expression in Rob and Ros's face whenever they looked at each other. She had heard from Lisa about the problems the couple were facing. Arla had been lucky with Harry, their little romance had blossomed into a relationship. But when it didn't work out, work place romances were the worst kind of romantic liaisons.

"Go home, all of you," Arla said. "It's been a long day."

"What about you, guv?" Lisa asked. "You look knackered, if you don't mind me saying."

"Oh thanks," Arla laughed. "No, I'm alright. I just need to be here till I hear more from DI Sanderson about Brian. I'll see you lot tomorrow."

CHAPTER 31

Lord Daniel Underwood relished the burn of the whisky as it slid down his throat. A 22-year-old bottle of Macallan, it didn't get much better than that. He stared at the ice in the tumbler, winking in the soft light of his study.

Older things were better, in general. Take the wisdom of older men, for instance. His mother had inherited some money, and she listened to his father, Adrian, when he suggested they invest the money in London's property marker. That was back in 1984. Adrian started buying land south of the Thames, where land was cheaper. He bought acres, and built houses and apartments. As London's economy boomed, so did the demand for housing.

Daniel took over the reins in the early nineties, by which time Underwood Property was worth close to a billion pounds in net asset value. Guided by Adrian, Daniel focused on the East End, and derelict industrial areas of North London. The canals around Islington and King's Cross were ripe for development, as they were occupied by the rusting hulk of warehouses that were no longer used.

In the Victorian times, barges floated down the canal, supplying raw materials and goods to the warehouses. But as roads and cars developed, the canals became useless as industrial pipelines. Hence the warehouses rotted, and clever property developers seized the opportunity for Canalside Living – as they called it.

Daniel smiled to himself. In the early 2000s, He made the most money building flats along the canals in north London. He never forgot his father's political connections, and he donated a third of that money to the Conservative Party, who looked after him with land grants, labour disputes. It was ironic, he thought. His father was a staunch Labour supporter, but he didn't blink an eyelid when Daniel went over to the Tories. When it came to money, all political parties were the same.

The door to his study opened, and his sister entered. Cora Underwood walked up to his sprawling desk, and he got up to peck her on the cheeks. He had been expecting her.

"Drink?" Daniel held up a whisky. "Looks like you need one." He grinned.

"Yes. But not that vile stuff. Have you got any rum?"

"Yes." Daniel went to his drinks cupboard and poured Cora a tall glass of rum and coke, and put a cherry in a toothpick on the top.

"Thanks," Cora took a sip, and rested her head back on the deep sofa. Daniel edged a footstool towards her and Cora put her legs on it.

Daniel sat down opposite her, on an armchair that had his name embossed on the back. He was close to Cora. He was proud of what she had achieved – a successful lawyer, who had become a Member of Parliament. Cora had given the family the respect that Adrian had craved all his life. Money brought respect, of course. Just like it bought power. But to have a politician in the family – that was a game changer. With any luck, Cora would one day be a cabinet member in a ruling government. Daniel hoped his father would be alive to see the day. After what the family had been through…it had to be worth it.

"Are you alright?" Daniel asked. "You sounded stressed on the phone."

Cora blew away a strand of hair that had fallen over her face. "I am. Well, kind of. It's about something that happened a long time ago. Richard called me."

"Richard…"

"Our cousin, Richard McPherson."

"Ah." Daniel sat back on the chair, his face impassive, but a turbulence now creeping across his mind. "What did he want?"

Daniel and Adrian had spent a lifetime distancing themselves from their cousins. It didn't work. After all, it was the family's money that started Adrian's property business. Money from the Cricklewood Crime Syndicate.

Cora took a long sip of the rum, and composed herself. Then she told Daniel. He stared at her disbelievingly. He reached for his tumbler of whisky and drained it.

"How far have the police got with this? Has it come back to you?"

"Not yet. But I get the feeling they're getting closer. Richard did something stupid. He got his men to attack an Inspector when they went to look for an informer in Slough. This man knew about Rachel. Now the cops have their hackles up."

Daniel swore under his breath. "He was always hot headed." He glanced at his sister, who was sitting up now, glass held in her hand. She took a sip, and put it on the table.

Daniel asked, "You've got a by election coming up, haven't you?"

"Yes. In two weeks. I need this like a hole in the head. And it's bad for business in general. I'm worried if Richard gets dragged into this, then so do we. In fact, Richard already is a suspect. I spoke to Melissa, one of Rachel's friends. She's a KC barrister now. She says there's no evidence to link back to Richard. But I'm not so sure. I don't trust this Detective Arla Baker. She's on a mission, and the whole mess has got a hundred times worse after what happened in Slough, when the inspector was attacked."

"Let me speak to Richard," Daniel said. "This should blow over, I think. I mean, it happened almost thirty years ago. Can you hold up your end?"

"For now, yes. But I'm getting worried."

CHAPTER 32

Arla was exhausted when she got back home. As she walked in through the door, she got a text from Nicole. The teenager was having fun in Dorset, and had posted a photo of herself with her friends by the campfire. Arla sent a heart emoji back, and the usual motherly advice about being careful.

Harry came over and gave her a peck on the cheek. As he straightened, he winced.

“Still hurting?” Arla asked, as she followed him into the kitchen. Harry ducked as he entered, his head was always slightly above the door frame.

“Its fine. I just got bored today. My boss sent me home for no reason.” He narrowed his eyes at Arla.

“Good job you didn’t stay,” Arla said, flopping on the dining table seat. Harry poured her a glass of red wine, and she accepted it with thanks.

“Is this about Brian Copeland? You chased him but he got away.”

Arla had chatted to Harry briefly, in the hope he or his contacts might know where Brian might head to.

"Yes, he did. Greg was helpful, he's good at his job."

"The Special Branch DI?"

"Yes. I should've listened to him and not given the order to approach Brian."

They were quiet for a while. Arla felt Harry's eyes on her. His voice was soft. "I'm alright, you know? And it's going to be fine. Don't worry."

Arla sighed, and said nothing. Harry said, "Don't rush into this because you're angry and feel you need to do something." He raised a hand, silencing her. "I don't mean that in a bad way." He leaned forward and pecked her on the lips. Arla kissed him back, her hand lingering on his face, sliding down the rough stubble on his cheek.

"Maybe I read the whole thing wrong," Arla said. "You should never have contacted Brian. I shouldn't have asked you."

"You asking me wasn't a bad move. Me telling Brian that we were investigating Rachel Mathew's death – that wasn't very clever. But he wouldn't give me much until I told him the reason for my call."

"You had no choice," Arla said. She took a long sip of the wine. It was a good red, she could taste the black cherries, and hints of liquorice. It was helping to numb the pounding in her brain. She rose and they went to the sitting room, where they could put their feet up on the sofa.

"I need to speak to Mike Boland once again," Arla said, once they were comfortable. "He must know something about McPherson's involvement."

"If Brian Copelan ran the way he did, I doubt Boland will mention anything else. It's also possible McPherson maintains contact with Boland. He's definitely hiding the truth, but how far will you get with him? He was cleared by the ACU."

"Just goes to show the ACU doesn't get hold of all the bent cops," Arla shook her head, frustrated. "Boland's probably been in McPherson's pay his whole life."

They were quiet for a while. Arla didn't like bringing her work home. But when her husband was a DI who worked with her – it was sometimes inevitable.

"What Barnaby confessed to was shocking," Arla said. "Do you think McPherson did that to Rachel?"

Harry frowned. "He doesn't have that sort of history. Did you ask Greg?"

"He agrees with you. He doesn't think McPherson has a fetish for that sort of torture." Arla shivered. "That sounds so…gross."

"Barnaby remains a suspect, right?" Harry said. "He could very well have killed Rachel."

"Yes. Lisa and Rob had a different feeling though. They don't think he was trying to throw them off scent."

“He worked for McPherson as an errand boy. Got arrested for it. Why would he admit to anything?” Harry poured some red wine into his glass, and Arla held out her glass too.

“He told us about the man Rachel was seeing. Whether it was McPherson or not, remains to be seen. But why would Barnaby even give us that, if he killed Rachel?” Arla shook her head. “We don’t know. But something tells me Barnaby wants nothing to do with this. He just wants to get out of prison to see his grandchild.”

Harry shrugged, and said nothing. The wine had drawn Arla into a warm, fuzzy zone, and she felt more relaxed. As she stared back at Harry, she thought about the years she had spent with him, and the family they had become. And what happened yesterday had brought her dangerously close to see that beautiful dream suddenly rupture like a bursting bubble. Arla had never thought she could sustain a relationship, never mind a long lasting one. But Harry had proved her wrong. Now, with Nicole, she couldn’t let go of Harry. She needed him.

“Harry?” She nudged him her foot. It rested on his lap, and he was stroking it. He looked up at her quizzically, recognising the change of tone in her voice. His large chestnut eyes were melting, and his light coffee coloured skin seemed to shine in the dim light from the table lamp.

“I need to tell you something.”

He held eyes with her. “Sounds serious.”

Arla let out a pent breath. She had to tell him. It was better out in the open than festering in her heart.

“I don’t want you to finish the AFO training. Stay with the SCU.” The Serious Crime Unit was where Arla worked.

Harry closed his eyes and tilted his head back. He massaged his forehead.

“Please, Harry,” Arla said, not liking the pleading sound in her voice. She felt as conflicted as a woman about to jump with a parachute from an aeroplane, but one who had a morbid fear of heights.

“I’ve put all this time and effort into this, and you know it. I’m about to finish the training.” Harry didn’t look at her.

“I know,” Arla said. “And you’ve known how I feel. What happened yesterday-

“Could’ve happened any day,” Harry said, his voice rising. “It’s the risk we accept when we sign up to our job. Every day we take a similar risk.” Harry shook his head, and Arla could see the anger in his tightly clenched jaws.

He was right, of course. But…Arla sighed. “I know. But is there any point in making that risk even worse? You could be in a firefight with terrorists, or armed robbers. Just think, Harry. You’ve got Nicole to think about now. What if something happens to me one day? Then you have to look after Nicole on your own."

"Oh god," Harry exhaled. He pushed Arla's feet away from his lap and stood. He walked to the patio doors that looked out over the garden of their ground floor flat. It was dark outside, and Arla saw Harry reflected in the glass. He looked troubled. She stood and went over to him.

"I'm sorry. What happened yesterday just shook me up. It's just made me more anxious, that's all."

Harry put his long arm around her shoulder and drew her into his comforting embrace. She succumbed to the warmth, cherishing the feel of his body. She put an arm around his waist.

"I don't want to lose you," she said. Emotion rose up in her throat, and she felt tears prickling the back of her eyes.

Harry kissed the top of her head. "You're not going to, silly. Stop worrying."

"Please tell me you'll think about it."

She felt him stiffen. His arms loosened around her shoulder. "I don't want to, Arla. I enjoy it. I want to finish the training." He put both hands on her shoulders, and looked into her eyes.

"It's going to be alright. Okay?"

What choice did Arla have? To her mind, he could at least consider it. Or was she being selfish?

She nodded, not saying anything. Harry kissed her forehead. She wanted to hold on to him, never let him go. He pulled her into a hug and she held on, tightly.

"There's something I had to tell you, as well."

She craned her head up at him. "Really? What?"

"While I was at home, I decided to look up missing persons to see if there was anyone else in North London like Rachel, who vanished around the same time."

Arla blinked. The last two days had been so busy the thought had escaped her mind. "I should've done that."

Harry smiled. "You can't do everything, right? But I guess you'll never stop trying. Anyway, I did find another person, as it happens. But not on the MPU." The MPU was the missing persons unit, UK's national database, run by the National Crime Agency.

They went back to the sofa and sat down. Harry said, "As you say, an absence of evidence is not evidence of absence." They both smiled.

"The year before Rachel vanished, in 1997, a female sex worker put in a PCN about a man who had physically abused her. She described the man as IC1, tall, thin, with glasses and smooth shaven. I read the PCN report." In the dimness of the room, Arla saw

Harry's face become serious. "This man tortured the sex worker. She was drugged, and he put hooks on her back, after injecting her to make the hooks less painful. He strung her up, and dangled her from the ceiling. She reported his room as being like a torture museum – with framed newspaper articles, old instruments of torture. I've sent you the reports."

Arla felt blood draining away from her body, leaving her cold and shaky. "Just as Barnaby described."

"Yes. The woman didn't remember the address, and she was drugged after she got into the man's car. He had taken her into the Hampstead Heath woods later on, presumably to kill her. But she managed to jump out of the moving car, and get away. The police investigated, but found nothing in Hampstead Heath."

"What happened to the woman?"

"I've got her name and details. But the phone number doesn't work. We need to search her tomorrow. She wasn't the only one. Another sex worker complained of a man with a similar description who tried to strangle her in his car, when she refused to drink, or be injected. She suspected he was trying to sedate her. She sprayed mace in his face, and escaped from the stationary car."

"And nothing came of it?"

"No. This guy turns up again, in 2000 in the same location, in Islington. Guess who went missing?"

“Another sex worker,” Arla whispered. “The women on the streets, and no one cares about them.”

“That’s right. A sex worker reported her friend missing, and she described the same type of man – tall, thin, glasses, IC1. The body was never found, and this person didn’t make it to the MPU.”

“It wasn’t compulsory in 2000,” Arla said. She got up, suddenly restless. “That’s when this sicko was active. God knows how many sex workers he killed, women who had no homes, drug addicts, no family and who were never reported missing.”

“Exactly. And all of this happened around Islington.”

Arla whirled around to face Harry. “But why did he let Rachel go? She told Barnaby what this man did to her.”

Harry shook his head. “I don’t know. And don’t ask me why, but I think this guy’s still out there.”

CHAPTER 33

Julia Slater locked up her office in Bexleyheath, and said goodbye to the receptionists at the front. The summer evening had turned to dark now, and she'd been in the office till way past closing time. It was nine pm now, and she was tired. Her conversation with Kate kept revolving in her mind like a psychotic hamster in a wheel.

The police were suspicious, that much Julia could tell. The same two detectives who came to see her, had also interrogated Kate. And Kate was the goody two shoes type. She always believed in telling the truth. What did that stupid bitch tell the police?

Julia's distraction had delayed her appointments, and hence she finished late. She hurried towards the bus stop, and decided to take a short cut through the park. The park was well lit, and there were other people on it. But the road it emerged into was dark, and quiet. Julia hurried on, she wanted to get home.

She didn't notice the man who'd been following her. She didn't see him till he got closer. She felt a presence behind her, and she gasped as a shadow appeared to her right. She jerked backwards, fear lashing against her spine. It was a man in a hoodie, and he stood there in silence watching her. Slowly, he removed the hoody, and he lit up his phone, pointing to his face.

"Chris?" Julia gasped. "What're you doing here…" she looked around. The street was empty. "How did you know I was here?"

The man stepped closer, and Julia went back. "I'll scream," she said, her heart hammering against her ribs, mouth dry. "Don't come closer."

"Oh, Julia," Chris smiled, spreading his hands. "Why're you scared of me? We used to be friends. I just want to talk."

"About what?"

"You know what. The police have been talking to you, haven't they? They found Rachel."

There was no point in denying it. Julia knew men like Chris were well connected. They would find out, sooner or later.

"Yes, they did. I told them I knew nothing. I only reported her missing."

"I see. Well, the police have been asking other people as well. I wonder how they knew about these people."

“I didn’t tell the police anything. I swear.” Despite her surging fear, Julia was interested. “Who are these people?”

“Remember Cora Underwood?”

Julia’s lungs froze, and she couldn’t breathe. “I didn’t tell the police anything about her, or anyone else. The police only know about me, Melissa and Kate.”

“Ah yes, Kate. Where is she these days? Hard woman to track down.”

Julia said nothing. She clutched the strap of her handbag. “I don’t know. I’ve got to go now.”

She turned to leave but Chris was quick, his hand a blur of movement as he reached out and grabbed Julia’s elbow. She screamed but he put a hand over her mouth, thrusting her against him.

“Don’t shout. Tell me where Kate is. I need to know.”

Julia struggled, but she knew it was no use. Her bulging eyes scanned the street, desperate to find a pedestrian. But it was empty.

Chris dragged her into the bushes on the sides of the street, and pushed her against a tree. Julia felt the rough bark against her neck, digging into her scalp.

“If you don’t tell me, I’ll finish you here. Then I’ll come after your parents in Swindon. Do you understand?”

Julia felt bitter bile rising in her throat, nausea suffusing her guts. Chris tightened his grip on her throat.

"Now then. Tell me where Kate is."

Julia couldn't speak, so he eased the pressure of his fist on her throat. Julia coughed and spluttered, then heaved on the ground. Chris grabbed the back of her coat, and pulled her up.

"Enough. Tell me now."

"In Broadstairs," Julia said, tears trickling down her eyes. "That's where she is."

"And what did she tell the police? I know she was the closest to Rachel. Rachel told her everything, didn't she?"

"I don't know."

"Don't lie. I know you three have been speaking to one another."

"I promise," fear made Julia's voice strident. From the corner of her eyes, she saw a man come into view, walking his dog. Chris leaned into her, pretending to kiss her. Julia closed her eyes, revolted by the smell of his sweaty body.

"I'll be in touch," Chris whispered in her ears. "Don't tell anyone you saw me. If you do, you know what happens."

CHAPTER 34

Arla didn't sleep well that night. What Harry had discovered stayed on her mind. The more she thought about it, the more sense it made. She didn't know if this man was alive anymore. But he could be, and if he was prowling around, preying on vulnerable women whom no one reported missing – he could've killed hundreds.

Arla got up at half four in the morning. Harry was still sound asleep. His back rose and fell as he breathed. Arla kissed him lightly on the shoulder, then got up. She got changed into her running gear. At five am, she was out on the streets of Tooting, which were still quiet. She ran to the open spaces of Tooting Common, her body warming up, her legs moving in synchrony with her breathing. She returned by six am, had a shower and got changed into her working clothes. She sat down with the reports that Harry had sent her.

All three of the women who had submitted the PCN's were sex workers in King's Cross station, which, in the 1990s, was well known as London's Red-Light District. The woman who had been taken to the man's house mentioned it not being too far – but she was blindfolded. She thought it was a game at first. After she was sedated by a spiked drink, she had little recollection of where she was, but she remembered her ordeal.

Arla felt the hairs rising on the back of her neck. This sick bastard actually kept memorabilia of serial killers? And instruments that were used to torture women in sado masochism?

Arla took out a map of London. She zoomed in on North London, and matched the locations on the reports to the current case. Regent's Canal, where Rachel was found, wasn't far from Hampstead Heath. Cricklewood, the area where McPherson's OCN used to be active, was also close by. Using both her hands and fingers, she traced a triangle on her phone map.

The apex was at Hampstead Heath, and the narrow base of the triangle was between Cricklewood and Angel tube station in Islington. In the triangle area, lay some of London's prized real estate. This used to be a run down, impoverished, crime ridden hell hole. But it all started to change in the early 2000s. Now the place was fully of swanky boutiques, art galleries, retro cafés, and the new flats sold for eye watering amounts. But Cricklewood hadn't changed much. It had a lot of social or council owned housing, and some of its streets remained as impoverished as decades ago.

Old secrets still festered in its narrow streets. Arla took a screenshot of her triangle, and sent it to Harry and Lisa. Harry was having another day at home, and he was still in bed when she left home at quarter to seven. She took the tube to work, enjoying the walk-through Clapham Common as usual.

She got her coffee from the canteen, and walked through to her office. The night duty team was leaving, and she got an update from them. No reports from DI Sanderson about Brian Copeland.

Arla walked through the open plan detective's section, which was filling up slowly. None of her team had arrived. She walked to the large map of London on the back wall. She noticed Hampstead Heath was not that close to Islington, but neither was it far. Less than ten miles. The Heath was a bastion of the well to do and affluent, and so were the areas surrounding it. But like all open areas in London, at night the reality was different. Arla wondered how many women this man had taken to the Heath, and how many he had killed.

The Heath was huge, and Arla knew searching it on her hunch would never happen. She needed a higher authority, and hence she called Johnson. To her surprise, her boss was in his fourth floor office. Arla went up the stairs, and knocked on the door. Johnson was in his Assistant Commissioners black and white uniform, which meant he had some media commitments later in the day.

"It's about the human remains we found in Regent's Canal, sir. The missing girl, Rachel Mathews. I have new evidence that this might have been the work of an unknown criminal who's been active in North London for years."

Arla told Johnson about what Harry had found, and that a search in Hampstead Heath might be useful.

"We can contact the women who submitted the PCN's. We can take them to the Heath if necessary."

"And what are you hoping to find, after almost thirty years? A mass burial ground? Be realistic, Arla."

"I know it's a needle in a haystack, sir. But I think these crimes are all linked. The MO is the same. He picks up the women, sedates them with drugs, then commits acts of torture and forced sex. He lets go of some, it seems, or they escape. He could've killed a lot more, sir."

Johnson was silent for a while. His massive hands rested on the table, then rose to form a steeple in front of his face.

"It's true that we underestimate the true extent of a serial killer's crimes. But in this case, the link is not proven, Arla. You have Rachel Mathews, and three PCN's – that's it. That's not good enough to start a search of a massive parkland like Hampton Heath." Johnson shook his head. "Sorry, that's not going to work."

Arla had thought so, but another idea had formed in her mind. She could always track down the sex workers, and take them to the crime scene herself.

She said, "There's another angle here, sir. We believe our killer had connections with the Cricklewood OCN in the 1990s. McPherson is running scared. You know what happened to Harry."

Concern rippled across Johnson's face. "I'm sorry, I forgot to ask you. How is he?"

"He's fine. It's him who found these PCN's and helped me to make the link."

Johnson pondered for a few seconds. "Well, keep searching for more victims. You've got a hard job, after all these years. Any forensics?"

"We have two DNA profiles from a man and woman who visited Rachel's flat. We should have more evidence from the tarpaulin and the crime scene."

"What's the criminal's connection to the OCN's?" Johnson stood and clasped his hands behind his back. He was a mountain of a man, rising to almost the ceiling. "I mean, why are they so fussed about this?"

"We don't know if McPherson's the killer. That would explain a lot, but we have his DNA on record from previous arrests. There's no match at the crime scene."

"What about his friends and associates?"

"You mean his partners at the OCN? None so far, either. It could be an unknown associate." Arla shook her head. The image of Harry almost getting shot was imprinted in her mind.

"Can I bring him? McPherson, I mean. I know his lawyer's will kick up a fuss. But surely, we have a right to at least question him."

"Yes, arresting him might be hard, but you can talk to him. Do it, and if you need help, let me know."

Well, Arla thought, that was refreshing. Normally, her discussions with Johnson ended up in an argument. She suspected he was sympathetic because of what happened to Harry. She thanked him, and went to her office.

Lisa and Gita had arrived, and Lisa strode up to her as she entered the open plan office. Lisa's face was tight with tension, her eyes glinting.

"You won't believe what I just heard, guv."

CHAPTER 35

"Brian Copeland was found dead inside a flat in the Greyfriars Estate in Cricklewood," Lisa said. They were in Arla's office, and Gita shut the door behind them.

Arla felt like she'd been slapped. Shockwaves erupted in her brain, pounding against her skull. She leaned against a filing cabinet, and stared at the floor, processing what Lisa said.

Lisa continued. "A resident on the fourth floor of the estate noticed a door that was open. She knew the flat was unoccupied, so she went in. A man was lying on the floor, and he'd been shot through the head."

Arla looked up. "Who informed you?"

"DI Sanderson from the Islington office. He said he's told Greg Warren, who's on his way. Apparently, he's tried to call you."

Arla didn't have any missed calls, but she was too distracted to check her phone right now.

"When were uniforms notified of the crime?"

"At six thirty am. The resident called 999. DI Sanderson was on duty, and his sergeant was on site by seven am. He identified the body, as they had photos of Copeland on their phones."

"Right, that does it," Arla straightened. "Bring Richard McPherson in for questioning. Brian Copeland was his known associate and was going to see him when he pulled Brian up. Later, Brian turns up dead. If that's not related, I don't know what is."

"Do we have ground for arrest?" Gita asked. "Suspect to murder?"

"Yes," Arla nodded. "I'm going to radio DI Sanderson now. Work with his team, and bring McPherson down here."

There was a knock on the door and Rob and Ros entered. To Arla, Rob looked subdued again. Ros separated from him, and stood next to Gita, while Rob sat down. Their body language didn't look good, and Arla suspected their relationship was over. She would have to speak to them later.

She bought the team up to speed on Harry's findings. Lisa looked at her phone. "I saw the map you sent me. You think this guy was active in that triangle? Then what about Regent's Park. That's also close by."

"Yes, we could look there too," Arla said. "But Johnson is right. Looking in the parks will be a nightmare. Lets track down these women. I want you guys to go through all cold cases with a similar MO, and description of the attacker. Any missing persons from that time, or in that area at any time, I want to know. Draw up a list of victims, and make contact with them today."

The team made their notes. Gita looked up. "Guv, I've been thinking. If Rachel confided in Barnaby, why wouldn't she tell her friends? I mean the ones close to her – Julia, Melissa and Kate."

Ros chimed in. "I was thinking the same. Kate especially, because she confessed to Rachel's peculiar sexual preferences. I think Rachel was closer to her, than to the other two."

"I agree," Arla said. "The dynamic between the friends is definitely weird. Can we bring Kate in for questioning? If she declines, can one of you go to see her?"

Ros and Gita looked at each other, and nodded at Arla. Ros said, "We can go again guv, no problems."

Arla got busy with answering emails and sorting out her intray as the team filed outside. She got a call from Dr Banerjee.

"I was hoping to hear from you," Arla said. "Things have been hectic here." She brought Dr Banerjee up to speed. Arla had worked with Dr B for decades, and the old man was like a father figure to her.

"Hmm. It seems whoever killed Rachel had a significant connection to the crime family. Perhaps a family member? Unless it was the boss himself."

"McPherson? Maybe. But it's a good point about a family member. Maybe that's why they're so rattled about a case from thirty years ago."

Family…Arla knew about McPherson's family, of course. He came from Ireland with his brother, and they took over the Cricklewood area's criminal activity. From there, the Irish gangsters spread across London. Richard had a brother, who was now in jail. But did Arla know about the rest of the family?

She pulled out her notepad, and wrote the word, then circled it twice.

Dr Banerjee said, "Maureen came back with her findings yesterday. She told me to call you, and you can speak to her as well, if you want."

"I will. But what did she find?" Prof Maureen Robinson was Dr Banerjee's partner.

"Well, its interesting. It's so small that I missed it, and so did my younger assistant. But the MRI scan at Maureen's unit picked it up. A tiny piece of cotton, no more than an inch in diameter. Maureen managed to blow it up with the magnifier. It shows a pattern of circles, each going into one another."

The memory hit Arla like a sledgehammer. "Like a Venn diagram, you mean? But instead of one circle, there's several."

"Exactly. A distinctive pattern, and it reminded me of something I'd seen before, but I can't be sure. Shall I send it to you now?"

"Yes please."

Moments later, Arla's' phone pinged with a message. She stared at the image – it was an exact replica of what she'd seen on the scarf in Rachel's wardrobe.

Circles were spinning in Arla's mind, coalescing into one another. This was the pattern she had seen on the scarf and cuff links in Rachel's wardrobe up North. A man's scarf and cuff links, one that Rachel had carried North with her, for some reason. Or had the man been up North? But Sarah didn't mention a man visiting Rachel when she was there. Maybe Sarah didn't see her? Or the scarf simply stayed in Rachel's suitcase, and she left it up north?

Either way, Maureen's finding was significant. It proved Rachel's connection to the man whose clothes held that pattern.

Dr Banerjee was speaking again. "Maureen said the victim might have been wearing a sock that had that logo. Or something tied to her feet – which is a bit harder to imagine."

Arla said, "I've seen clothes with that logo in Rachel's possession, so a sock makes sense."

If it was a sock, did Rachel borrow it from someone, or was it put on her?

The sock was on Rachel when she died. Was it put in place by the man who killed her?

"Thanks, Doc. I'll speak to Maureen."

Arla hung up, and went outside. Rob waved at her. He was on the phone, and held it against his chest to silence it.

"McPherson's refusing to come out. He says they need a search warrant to enter his house, which uniforms don't have. I've got DI Sanderson on the line."

Arla extended her hand, and Rob gave her the phone. Arla spoke into it. "DCI Baker."

"Hi, DI Sanderson here. Richard McPherson has sent us word he has no wish to speak to us. He's a free citizen, and if we want to speak, or arrest him, we need to enter his house. And he won't give us permission to do that."

"How is he contacting you?"

"Through his lawyers."

Arla thought for a second. "Send me his lawyer's number, and tell them to expect my call."

Five minutes later, Arla was in her office, leaning back on her desk chair. James Slattery, McPherson's solicitor, was on the line.

"DCI Baker, is it?"

"Yes. We need to speak to your client urgently about the murder of his associate Brian Copeland."

"My client does not know anyone by that name."

"He was going to see your client yesterday. How can he not know him?"

"How do you know Mr Copeland wasn't going somewhere else?"

Arla knew this game well. She didn't have time for it. "Tell your client we will alert the media as part of our search for witnesses to the murder victim. Mr Copeland's gang links will be tomorrow's headlines. I can see them already. *Crime Boss living stone's throw from where his old pal was murdered.*" Arla paused. "Richard McPherson's name would be in the papers. Would your client like that?"

Slattery was silent. When he didn't respond, Arla said, "Alright, then. We will alert the media, and we're holding a press conference today as well. We won't hold Mr McPherson's name from the reporters. Goodbye."

"Hold on. Can I call you back in ten minutes."

"Make it five," Arla said, and hung up. It took two minutes for Mr Slattery to call Arla back.

"My client will see you at his home."

"I thought he might."

CHAPTER 36

There was a knock on Arla's door, and DI Greg Warren entered. "I heard," he said, standing opposite her desk. "Unbelievable news. DI Sanderson's team has the estate under lockdown. There will be CCTV footage of the attacker. Plenty of cameras up there. Whoever did this took one hell of a risk."

"Which is why we're going to pay Mr McPherson a visit." Arla told Greg about her conversation with Mr Slattery. Greg grinned at her.

"You did well there. I've come across that Mr Slattery before. Absolute arsehole."

"Perfect term for a highly paid solicitor," Arla said, rising. "One who protects criminals, anyway." Arla collected her warrant card, and as an afterthought, also her extendable steel baton.

Greg raised his eyebrows. "Expecting trouble?"

"That's why you're coming with me," Arla said.

Greg was surprised. "Me? But…"

"Getting cold feet?" Arla smiled. "Only joking. I need a witness with me. I can take one of my sergeants, as DI Mehta isn't here. But I thought you might want to meet Mr McPherson."

"Let me speak to my boss," Greg said.

Arla nodded. "I'll be out in the car park."

Greg joined her outside. His boss had agreed for him to attend, and Greg drove the car back to the street where they had last seen Brian Copeland. This time, there was a police guard outside the door of McPherson's house.

Arla and Greg rang the doorbell. A swarthy, barrel-chested man who looked straight out of a Hollywood mafia gangster movie opened the door. He was even wearing a black suit. Arla half expected him to speak in a downtown New York accent. But he said nothing.

Arla and Greg held up their warrant cards, and the man grunted. He turned and then went up the stairs. Arla followed. The living room on the first floor was large and spacious, and if there was a style of decoration called gangster chic – then this was it. The entire room was panelled with dark wood, and the floor was the same, with a couple of white rugs. Two huge dark red leather chesterfield sofas stood in the corners, with a black coffee table in the middle. There was a fireplace, and above that, a massive mirror. A tiger skin was stretched on the wall, complete with the head and fangs. If that was an original – and it looked like the real thing – it would've cost a bomb. A chandelier hung from the high ceiling; it's crystal light illuminating the room.

Arla felt like she had stepped into a film set of the Godfather. Mr McPherson turned around from the window, and approached them. He had a tight smile on his face, his blue eyes watchful. His skin was tanned to leather, white hair swept back from his forehead. When he smiled, his teeth dazzled. He was a good-looking man who had kept himself in great shape, Arla had to admit. He must be past sixty, but carried himself light on his feet, the stance and gait of a much younger man.

"Inspector Baker," he said slowly, holding her hand for longer than necessary. A cloud of fragrant aftershave assaulted Arla's nostrils. Did he just pour the bottle over himself?

"I've heard so much about you. So nice of you to come to see me." He stretched an arm to the sofa. "Please have a seat." He nodded at Greg, and then moved to the other sofa.

Arla denied the offer of tea or coffee. The steroid pumped, black suited goon from downstairs took his place at the door, his eyes on them.

McPherson said, "Inspector Baker, I don't have any female employees today, hence I am not going to search you. But if you are carrying a weapon, would you please put it on the table?"

Charming and suave, Arla thought. But that wouldn't get him on her good side. She nodded, and put her baton on the table. Greg lifted both hands. "I don't have anything on me. But you can search me if you wish."

The goon came forward, and Greg stood. He was patted down, and Arla noted another man at the door, standing just out of sight. She could see his feet. He moved, and came into view briefly, then disappeared again. The man who searched Greg took his position at the door.

Steps sounded, and Arla looked up to see a man in an expensive pin striped suit come into the room. He was short, with cold, appraising eyes, and a smile that was fixed on his lips like a sticking plaster. Arla knew who he was before McPherson introduced him.

"This is my lawyer, Mr Slattery. You don't mind if he sits with us?"

He didn't wait for Arla's acceptance. Mr Slattery sat down next to McPherson, and took out a notebook, and a small device. Arla glanced at it.

"This conversation should not be recorded," Arla said, staring at Slattery first, then at McPherson. "If that's what you want, we can have the conversation at the station."

Slattery went to speak, but McPherson raised a hand. Reluctantly, Slattery put the device away.

"Take the batteries out please," Arla said. Slattery looked at Arla as if she'd just asked him to get up and dance the tango. Then he sighed, shook his head, and took the batteries out of the device. He held them up.

"There you go. Happy?"

"Thank you," Arla said. She looked back at McPherson, who was sitting back on the sofa, and stroking his chin as he observed her.

Arla said, "So you must know the purpose of our visit. One of your colleagues was coming to see you yesterday. We stopped him, and he ran away. This morning, we found him dead in an unoccupied flat less than two miles from here. His name was Brian Copeland. We went to see him in Slough, because we thought he had some information about a case involving a murder victim from many years ago. Rachel Mathews."

Arla paused. McPherson remained relaxed. She continued. "We have proof that Copeland was an associate of yours from many years ago. He turned into an informer and he had witness protection. But we believe he had contact with you. Is that correct?"

McPherson smiled. "Inspector Baker, I'm afraid I don't know what this is about. I don't know any Brian Copeland."

Arla pulled out her phone, but didn't open it. She knew this from memory. "He worked for you in the late nineties. He transferred goods and weapons. He knew the Askey Boys in Finchley, a rival OCN to yours. He acted as a go between. Does that ring any bells?"

"Nope."

Arla had nothing to gain from this line of questioning, so she switched gears. "Why was Brian coming to see you yesterday?"

"I don't know who he is, so…" McPherson raised his shoulders, and waved a hand in the air, in denial.

"Did you know Mike Boland, a detective sergeant in the London Met?"

"No."

"He dealt with Rachel Mathew's disappearance, back in 1998. Speaking to him led us to you, and to Brian Copeland." Arla detected a tightness in McPherson's jaws. "Did you know Rachel Mathews?"

"No."

"Are you sure?" Arla held eyes with McPherson, and Slattery stirred, as if he wanted to say something.

"I'm sure, Inspector." McPherson smiled slightly, and the corners of his eyes crinkled.

"Then why did your men try to kill one of our Detective Inspectors when we went to question Mr Copeland in Slough?"

The smile remained on McPherson's face, but it was frozen, like the lips had forgotten how to move. He didn't speak for a few seconds. Then the smile widened again, but his expression was colder now, and more watchful.

"Again, I'm afraid I don't understand what you're talking about. I don't know a Mr Copeland, nor am I aware what happened to your DI." He raised his eyebrows. "Is the DI okay though? Terrible thing to happen to anyone."

Arla detected a fakeness in his concern, and a glimmer of delight seemed to dance across his eyes. Her jaws tightened, and her nostrils flared, but she kept herself in check. McPherson wasn't going to get a rise out of her.

"You were arrested twice. Then you left for Spain." Arla raised a hand as Slattery went to speak. "Yes, I know all charges against you were dropped. Why did you come back?"

McPherson seemed surprised. "I'm a free man, Inspector. I'm allowed to travel wherever I want to, is that not true?"

"I was wondering if there was a reason why you returned to London. Was it to take care of business."

"Yes." He spread his hands. "Look Inspector, like you, I'm busy. Is there anything else I can help you with?"

“Yes. Do you know Simon Barnaby?”

A shadow passed over McPherson’s face. He lowered his head, as if deep in thought. “Can’t say I do, Inspector. Why?”

“He’s in jail currently. He was another associate of yours. He knew Rachel Mathews, and dated her. He said she was physically abused by a man before her death. Do you know who this man might be?”

McPherson blinked a couple of times, and his lips downturned. But Arla could see the effort to keep his expression bland. His neck muscles were taut, and his fingers were curled up on his knees. His feet moved, like the Adams apple on his neck.

“I have no idea what you’re talking about, Inspector.”

Arla fixed him with a stare. “Are you into instruments of torture, Mr McPherson? For example, do you derive pleasure by sticking pins or needles into flesh? It’s a form of sado masochism.”

McPherson’s eyes blinked open. “I’m sorry. What do you mean?”

“It’s very simple. Do you believe in torturing women or not?”

“No, of course I don’t.”

Slattery cleared his throat. “Inspector, I really think this has gone far enough. These are frankly bizarre questions, and I don't believe you have any right to ask my client these."

Arla turned to him. "Well, it is clear that your client was involved with Rachel Mathews in some way"

She focused on McPherson again. "Brian Copeland tipped you off when we got in touch with him, hence your men attacked one of my DI's. Then Simon Barnaby turns out to be another one of your associates. Copeland is now dead. Can you see the line joining the dots?"

Slattery spoke again. "There is no line or angle here, DCI Baker. My client was gracious enough to grant you an interview. Now you are simply harassing him."

Arla ignored him, and stared at McPherson. "Do you have anything to say?"

"I've answered all your questions," he said stiffly. The smile was now fading and his jaws were lax. "I would like you to leave now, Inspector."

CHAPTER 37

From McPherson's house in Cricklewood, Arla and Greg visited the Greyfriars Estate. Greg parked the car outside the massive compound, which housed a collection of tall, slate grey buildings that housed the poor and dispossessed. Arla didn't get out immediately.

"Are you alright?" Greg said. "That was a heavy interview."

"He's hiding something," Arla said. She looked at Greg. "For the first time, I think he might well have done it. I wouldn't put it past him."

Greg grimaced. "Maybe. But that doesn't fit his record. He had a lot to lose in his criminal activities if he was caught doing weird crap like this."

"You don't think he's guilty of at least knowing Rachel?"

Greg leaned his head back on the car seat and appeared deep in thought. "I don't know. He might have known Rachel, but so far, we have no proof of that."

"Then who is he protecting, if not himself?"

"That remains the big question," Greg conceded. His fingers tapped the steering wheel.

Arla pressed her lips together. She needed some time alone.

"You go ahead, I'll lock the car and follow you."

Greg nodded and left the keys with her. Arla stared out the window, her mind going round slowly, trying to reach the centre of her rumination. She could see a shape here, and it was vague, but slowly getting clearer. She remembered what Dr Banerjee had said. She pulled out her phone and called Lisa. She had left instructions with Lisa before she left the nick this morning.

"Did you look up McPherson's family members?"

"Yes guv. His brother James is in prison, as you know. James has a son called Declan, who's in America with his family. Richard has a sister called Delia. Now Delia is interesting, but not for what you might think. No criminal connections with her, in fact it's the opposite."

"What do you mean?"

"Delia married an Englishman called Adrian Underwood, who happened to be a builder. Delia got some money from her brothers, because they needed to keep it safe, and it became her inheritance. So, with Adrian, Delia started a real estate business, back in the eighties. Have you heard of the Underwood Property Group?"

"Nope. Are they big?"

"Yes, as it happens. The website is impressive, and I made some enquiries with their competitors. The company spokesman didn't want to speak to me, as it happens."

Arla pressed her lips together, her eyes narrowing. "Adrian and Delia will be older now. Did they have any children?"

"Yes, two boys and a girl. Daniel, Cora and Chris. Daniel now runs the company. He's a big shot, as you can imagine. Chris I can't get much info on. I've got his passport and address – which is the same as his parents. He works for Underwood Property Group as an Administration Agent, according to their website. I have no idea what that job title means. But Cora is interesting."

Lisa paused. "She used to be a solicitor, but now she's an MP for Ealing, in west London. She's doing well in the Conservative Party, and has a shadow cabinet position in the Health Department. She's tipped to do well if the Tories win the next election."

Arla had her notebook out, and she was scribbling. "What's her full name?"

"Cora Underwood."

Arla wrote the names of all three siblings. She circled Daniel and Cora's names, and put a question mark next to Chris. Lisa continued.

"Cora is in a tight race for the West Ealing by Election in two weeks' time. She's campaigning a lot these days. She holds surgeries to meet her constituents at churches and community halls. We could meet up with her easily."

Arla felt that amorphous shape again, moving across her mind like a mirage in the desert. What was she missing here?

"Is there any evidence that the three children knew Rachel? They would be the same age."

"Yes, that's right. Cora is the youngest, and she's fifty three. Daniel is fifty eight, and Chris fifty five. But no, there's nothing to suggest they knew Rachel."

Arla thought for a while. "Have any of them been in contact with the police about Rachel in the past? Like, to report her missing."

"Nope, and no PCN's either. We're talking about a powerful family here, guv. They have hundreds of millions, and political connections."

"And it all started with gangster's money," Arla said softly. "Do you think that was a deliberate plan to divert funds to keep it clean?"

"I don't know, but if that was the plan, it seems to have worked. However, I looked through all of the

Underwood's – they have no links to the McPherson's." Lisa cleared her throat. "Almost as if they want to remain distant from them."

Arla smacked her forehead. She should've questioned McPherson about his extended family when she saw him. Even if she met a wall of no comment, it would've been interesting to see his response.

"Maybe the two sides of the family don't mix," Arla said. "They want to be kept separate from one another."

But the real buzz was now humming loudly in her brain, like an engine getting into gear.

"But now, with Rachel's case, they are thrust into this together. I think so, anyway, despite there not being any evidence that they knew Rachel."

She was thinking aloud. "If McPherson isn't acting to protect himself, what about one of his family members? Like one of the Underwood's. If their company is that big, it's worth protecting right?"

Arla thought of how Richard McPherson had evaded justice for so long, and how easily he had bought police officers in the past. Did his cousins political connections help? This was all conjecture right now, but it made Arla uneasy.

"That's what I was thinking as well, guv," Lisa said. "The Underwood Group is big. Huge, actually. Rob and I looked at the company's filings. Their gross revenue is close to a billion pounds last year. They're also big donors to the Conservative Party, but they also donate to Labour when they're in power."

"Yes. Money is blind to politics." Arla shook her head. How had she missed this? "Set up meetings with all three of them. If Cora will be the easiest to approach, then let's meet up with her first. I suggest we simply turn up and surprise her."

"Ooh, nice," Lisa giggled. "Can't wait to see her posh face when you ask her about her gangster uncle."

Arla grinned, and told Lisa to be ready for when she returned.

****

Arla locked the car, and walked down the wide courtyard, the colossal grey cement buildings looking down on her like giants. Thousands of people lived in these tiny flats, each window pane told a story. People from far flung corners of the world, and those who had nothing, not even their dreams. Black, white, brown, people of every shade of colour and nationality. Vibrant, and not subdued. They lived in harmony and eked out an existence in London's inner-city jungle. For Arla, this was the essence of London, not the areas where the silver tongued, empty bellied big wigs lived.

The crime scene was at the end of the huge courtyard. Arla crossed a mini shopping market, and a creche for babies. She saw the uniforms standing guard outside the block of flat. She showed her warrant card, and signed her name on the offered sheet. Then she took the lift up to the fourth floor. Uniforms also stood guard here, and a resident was asking a female constable when the barriers would lift. A door to door was in progress, and at the end of the long corridor, Arla could see uniformed officers speaking to a woman standing at the door to her flat.

The crime scene was busy. It was a small flat, and she bumped into a white coated scene of crime officer coming out. She put on her mask, gloves and shoe coverings. She stepped on the sterile boards placed on the floor. The windows were open, but the air was still hot and stuffy. Arla stopped at the door, and examined it, and the frame. No sign of a break and entry.

She went in through the narrow hallway, past two bedrooms and a bathroom, and into the main lounge. Large windows looked out over London's skyline. On the floor, the body lay face down. A bullet hole at the base of the neck had made a mess of the skull. Blood and brain tissue lay congealed around the skull bone fragments. Halogen lights lit up the body with vivid clarity. A scene of crimes officer was patiently taking swabs from the ground by the victim's feet. The victim was fully dressed in a light brown jacket and jeans. He had shoes on his feet. Greg was crouching by the head, and he stood when he saw Arla.

He lowered his mask when he shuffled closer. “This was a professional hit. One shot, from behind.”

“Have we found the bullet and cartridge?”

Greg shook his head. “No. I’m not sure if the bullet is still lodged in the skull. It might be. I can’t see an obvious exit wound. But the cartridge was picked up and discarded.”

Arla stepped around the body to have a closer look at the shattered skull. Her knowledge of gunshot wounds wasn’t huge, and she wished Harry was here. But she thought she could make out the exit wound. She pointed it to Greg, who shrugged. He pointed at the opposite wall.

“If he was shot here, facing the window, and his attacker was behind him, then an exit bullet would mark the wall.”

Arla glanced at the wall and he was right, there was no mark. She nodded. “Do you think the killer might have picked up the bullet, with the cartridge?”

“Possible, yes. He was a professional, I wouldn’t expect anything less.” He frowned as he rubbed his chin. “Who would’ve known he was here? It had to be one of McPherson’s men. This is one of their old stomping grounds. They still have eyes here.”

“There’s no sign of breaking and entering, and the windows facing the balcony are intact,” Arla said. “Copeland let his attacker come in. He knew that person. Had to be someone he trusted, because he was on the run from us.”

Greg spoke slowly. “His phone doesn’t show any signal from last night. He was using a burner phone. We can’t trace it. But you’re right. Copeland knew his killer.”

Greg indicated the flat. “I looked into the previous owners. This flat was raided by police in the past. It was used to stash cash, drugs and weapons, and the gangs paid the family who lived here. A cuckoo’s nest, in other words.”

Arla was familiar with the term. “Can you track down the previous resident?”

“Already have. I spoke to them, and they told me a couple of names. New gang members, in different gangs. But I can speak to one of my informers. I’m meeting up with them later today. They now live in White City, in another council estate.”

“Good,” Arla said, relieved. Greg was a senior intelligence officer, with deep contacts. She was glad he was working with her. He didn’t try to take over the investigation, or act bossy. He wasn’t like previous Special Branch DI’s she had known, and she appreciated that.

Greg said, “We’re also checking the CCTV as we speak. There’re loads of cameras here, it’s only a matter of time before we find the shooter.”

CHAPTER 38

Back in the Clapham nick, Lisa hurried over to Arla when she entered. Rob and Gita were at Lisa's desk as they approached.

"We've got some interesting news. Remember you told us to keep tabs on the phones of Rachels friends?"

"Yes," Arla said, sipping from a plastic cup of water she'd picked up.

"Melissa Carrington," Lisa said. "We checked her call list, and found she called Cora Underwood's office. The next call to Melissa was from a burner phone. The same burner phone also called Julia and Kate. The number was unidentified, but we erased the 1471 cover and got the digits." In UK, pressing 1471 before a phone number hid the caller's number. But it didn't hide it from the police.

"So, we think the burner phone belongs to Melissa? Have we triangulated the signal?"

Rob spoke up. "Yes, I just got the data. The calls were all made from Kensington Gore, near Hyde Park. The house is owned by the Underwood Property Group. We don't have anyone else's name."

Lisa smiled at Arla. "Looks like we know who called Rachel's friends. If not Cora, it could be one of her brothers."

"Yes," Arla said. "Kensington Gore is right next to Hyde Park, there's a gazillion cameras there. Can we check who goes in and out of that house?"

Gita said, "I can do that now, guv. I'll check with traffic."

Rob said, "A few interesting things about Melissa, guv. She's a high-flying barrister, but she used to work with Cora Underwood in the same firm. Cora was senior to her, and they worked in cases together. Hence, they know each other. I spoke to the senior partner at the firm just now. He says Cora helped Melissa get high value clients. It's one of the reasons Melissa did so well in her career."

Arla narrowed her eyes. "Does Cora have similar connections to Julia and Kate?"

Gita said, "Not that we can see, but it's almost certain that Cora spoke to them recently."

That shapeless mass in the middle of Arla's mind was moving, altering, changing like a living shape. For the first time she could see its structure, the eyes, nose, and the sharp fangs of a creature that had lain dormant for years. She breathed faster.

"Dig into Daniel and Chris. They are our two main suspects now. Find out everything you can about them."

Arla rubbed her hands together, and glanced at Lisa. "Good work. Keep tracking that burner phone. Let me know of any updates. Let's pay Miss Underwood a visit, shall we?"

***

Ealing, a leafy suburb in West London, was once a haunt of the glamorous and the cultural glitterati due to the proximity of the Pinewood Studios. James Bond's first films were shot in that iconic studio, and a host of other global hit films. These days, Ealing is a quieter residential area, but close to the bustling west end of London.

It was late afternoon when Lisa and Arla walked down the high street, heading for the Community Centre. Lisa had called up the local Conservative office, and they knew that Cora Underwood was still seeing her constituents at the centre. It was three pm on the dot, and Cora would be there for another hour.

A section of the Community Centre Hall had been partitioned for the surgery, as visits were called, with the MP. Arla and Lisa presented their names and jobs, and waited. After half an hour of waiting, and watching people who came after them leapfrog to the front, Arla had enough. Either Cora didn't know they were here, or she was avoiding them.

"Go around the back," Arla said. "Make sure she doesn't leave the via the rear car park."

Lisa left, and Arla went up to the man who was managing the constituents. She showed her warrant card again, and the man looked worried.

"Is everything okay, Detective? Is there a particular reason you want to see Ms Underwood?"

"Yes, and I can't wait any longer."

"Let me check." The man disappeared behind the partition and Arla heard whispered voices, then silence. A woman was helping the man, and she smiled at Arla uncertainly. The man returned, looking sheepish.

"Ms Underwood is currently busy in consultation with a school teacher, and she said-

"No," Arla said. "I need to see her now, or she can come to the station to speak to me officially."

The man's eyes widened, and his Adam's apple rose and fell. "I…" he glanced at his female colleague, who was gaping at him, and Arla. "If you could please wait for just another few minutes –

Arla pushed past the man, who put out an arm to stop her. Arla shoved his hand to one side, and the man gasped as if surprised by Arla's strength. Arla stormed into the chamber, and stalked up to the desk where a woman was sat with a couple opposite her. There was a man seated a discreet distance away, and Arla thought he was a bodyguard. The man rose and walked swiftly towards Arla.

"Get out of my sight," Arla raised a finger at the man, who she thought was Ex-Army. He moved light and swiftly on the balls of his feet. "Or I'm going to arrest you for harassing a police officer." She took out her warrant card and held it up to his astonished face.

"DCI Baker of the London Met. I'm here to speak to Miss Underwood."

Arla turned her attention to Cora. The woman was glaring at Arla. She was well dressed in an immaculate black pant suit, and white blouse. Her blonde hair cascaded to her shoulders, and the light brown highlights in them had been done by an expert hairdresser. She was in her fifties, and in excellent shape. The size ten suit fit her perfectly. Cora Underwood's eyes flashed once, and she turned to the couple seated in front of her.

"Would you mind giving me a minute, please. I'll see you again very shortly."

The couple nodded, and got up. They looked at Arla curiously as they left. Arla sat down in one of the chairs the couple had just vacated. Cora was beautiful, with large eyes that had light mascara, and grey pupils. Her cheeks were mottled with rage, and her lips were pressed so tight together they were turning white.

"DCI Baker," Arla said again. "Nice to meet you, Miss Underwood."

Cora squeezed her words out between teeth clenched so tight it seemed a single molecule of air wouldn't pass between them.

"To what do I owe this pleasure, Inspector Baker?"

"I've just been to see your uncle," Arla said airily, as if she was discussing the weather. She crossed her legs. "He's under suspicion for killing a man, and also implicated in the death of a woman you might well know. Rachel Mathews."

If Cora's eyes were lasers, Arla would've been burnt to crisp. Without moving her slicing gaze on Arla, Cora raised a hand.

"Adam, leave us alone. Make sure no one disturbs us."

The man coughed once, and strode out to comply with her orders. Arla smiled. "Thank you. Now we can speak openly."

"What do you want?"

"I want to know if you knew Rachel Mathews. It seems like you do."

"I'm afraid you're mistaken." Cora ground her teeth together. "So please stop wasting my time."

"Then why did Rachel's friend, Melissa Carrington, call you yesterday?"

Cora faltered, like a champion boxer who just got hit by a sucker punch on the face. She recovered in an instant.

"Are you spying on my phone, Inspector? That's not allowed, and you know it. Besides, it will never be admissible in court, if this ludicrous nonsense ever gets that far."

"I don't need anyone's permission to monitor the activities of murder suspects. If you don't know that, I suggest you look up PACE."

The Police and Criminal Evidence Act of 1984 underpinned the legal framework the police worked on.

Cora's delicate lips lifted upwards at the corner, and her nose crinkled like there was a bad smell in the room.

"I am a solicitor so of course I know what PACE is."

"Then you will know what I'm talking about. Can you please answer the question? Why did Melissa Carrington call you?"

Cora shrugged. "To talk about a case I dealt with many years ago. That was all."

"And then a burner phone called Melissa back. The burner phone also called Julia Slater and Kate Turner. This phone was traced back to a house in Kensington Gore. It's owned by Underwood Property Group – your father's company. Do you happen to live there, by any chance?"

This wasn't a punch on the chin, it was a sledgehammer to the solar plexus. Colour drained from Cora's face like sunlight on a winter's evening. A storm settled on her features, pressing her down. She swallowed, and her lips seemed to have trouble uttering words.

"I don't know what you're talking about, Miss Baker."

"DCI Baker, actually." Arla twisted the knife deeper. "Does that burner phone belong to you, Miss Underwood?"

"No comment."

Arla angled her head. "I'll take that as a yes, then. What did you tell Rachel's friends?"

Flecks of colour appeared on Cora's face, like drops of blood on snow. "Miss…DCI Baker. I'm not speaking to you without my solicitor present."

Arla had feared that, and she felt deflated. She had hoped to get more out of Cora. Well, there was no hiding anymore.

"Who are you protecting, Cora? Tell me his name."

Cora scraped her chair back, and stood. “Thank you, DCI Baker.”

Arla stood slowly. “Is it one of your brothers? Or your uncle?”

“Please leave now, Miss Baker.”

Arla leaned forward slightly. She dropped her voice to whisper.

“Do you know what Simon Barnaby, Rachel’s lover, told us? Rachel was with a man who loved to physically torture her. He stuck hooks on her back, dangled her from the ceiling, and cut into her flesh with knives and pins.”

If Arla had slapped Cora, she might have looked less shocked. Her lips parted, and her neck muscles contracted powerfully. The air turned into a solid, invisible mass, encapsulating them in a tense silence.

Arla’s words perforated the miasma. “Can you imagine how terrified Rachel must’ve been? And Rachel wasn’t the only one. We know several sex workers in North London who complained about a man who tortured them in the same way.”

Cora’s eyes widened in a rictus of fear, and she forgot to breathe, it seemed. Her chest bulged with lack of air.

“Tell me, Cora,” Arla whispered her name for the first time. “And I promise this won’t get back to you.”

Cora stood transfixed, as if hypnotised by Arla's words. She opened her mouth and gulped air. Then she blinked, and a shadow seemed to move past her eyes.

"Leave now, DCI Baker. Or I will call security."

CHAPTER 39

Kate Turner was having a nightmare finishing up her latest review. The manager and owner of a resort in Bali had got in touch with Jeff about the negative – as they saw it – review that Kate had done. In truth, the resort had a case of food poisoning when Kate visited last year, and some of the residents had been sick. The resort was lucky they were getting a review at all, and not a report to the Indonesian Health Authority.

Jeff called her in to his office and droned on for half an hour how she had to reword her review in the next edition of the magazine. Kate had refused so far, but Jeff was being insistent. The resorts paid good money to host the journalists, and paid for their flights.

Kate was still holding her ground, but the arguments were giving her a headache. She went back to her desk and opened and shut her drawers, looking for a hair tie. She slammed a drawer shut angrily when she couldn't find one. It wasn't on her wrist for some reason. Then she found it on the floor. As she tied her hair up in a ponytail, she saw a message on her screen. She had received an email.

Like every journalist, Kate handed out her card to all and sundry in the hope of getting a news scoop. Kate didn't work for a tabloid gossip magazine, but even in the lifestyle genre, there were always juicy titbits. Bad news sold more than good news. It was in every journalist's DNA to sniff out controversies and Kate was no different.

The email was from an anonymous person who had news about the Kent Council and sewage disposal. As it happened, some of the sea beaches in Broadstairs, and other parts of Kent – a county that had long sandy beaches – had been polluted by sewage recently. The residents had duly complained and the papers had picked it up. So this was an interesting topic.

She emailed back, asking for the person's name. They sent a phone number back and asked Kate to call. This was a business call, so Kate stayed in the office. She called the number. A man answered.

"Hello, this is Kate Turner from the Kentish Days magazine."

"Hello, Miss Turner. My name is Chris. Just call me Chris for now."

Must be a council worker, Kate thought. Maybe someone who had access to the contracts of the Council and the sewage disposal company. That's why he didn't want to disclose his full name.

"How can I help?" Kate asked. "You can speak freely. Your name or contact will never be disclosed in the media."

"Oh, that's good." The man was quiet for a while. "Shame what happened to Rachel all those years ago, eh?"

Blood drained from Kate's face. Her heart thumped loudly against her ribs. "Who…who is this?"

"Someone who cares about you, Kate. And also cared about Rachel."

Chris…the name hit her like the scream of a train engine in a tunnel. She couldn't breathe. Her chest was a block of ice.

"Chris, is that you?"

"Yes. Nice to speak to you after all these years."

"Don't call me again. I'm hanging up."

"Oh, come on. That's no way to speak to an old friend. Why don't we meet up and chat one day?"

"I'm not your friend. And I don't want to meet you."

A touch of hardness crept into Chris's voice. "What have you told the police?"

A jolt of fear sparked in Kate's heart. "Nothing."

"Really? Are you sure?"

"I'm hanging up. I don't want to speak to you anymore.

"That's a shame. How are your parents, by the way? Are they still living in the Wirral, near Merseyside?

22 Lancaster Avenue, isn't it? I've heard the Wirral is lovely. Might visit sometime."

The thorns were spreading tentacles into Kate's body, claiming her frozen limbs. Her guts felt hollow, like they'd been scooped out.

"You…leave my parents out of this." Kate pressed fingertips to her temples, and rested her elbow on the table.

"What do you want?"

"Just to meet, and talk. For old time's sake. Wouldn't that be nice?" Chris chuckled, a sound that spread like molten lava through Kate's ears. She wanted to say she'd go to the police, but she could guess the connections his family had with the police. She looked around her. Her colleagues weren't paying her any attention.

"When and where?" She wondered if he knew where she lived. But how could he? She'd taken care when she moved. She bought the property under her mother's name. The house bills were also paid from an account in her mother's name…is that how Chris found her?

Or did someone else tell him?

"I'll let you know."

The phone went dead, and Kate put it down slowly, as if it was an explosive device she had just neutralised.

CHAPTER 40

Cora stepped outside through the back door. She took a deep breath to steady herself. She leaned against the portico, trying to calm her nerves. Her life had flickered past her eyes when Arla Baker was talking. Visions of her childhood, her parents, her brother. She had reached an edge, and beyond it, lay a void. She couldn't see past that emptiness.

Cora knew she had to do something. She pulled out her phone and called Daniel. It went to voicemail, but he called her back while she was leaving a text.

"The police just came to see me at the surgery in Ealing. It was that detective, Arla Baker."

"My goodness," Daniel sighed. "What did she have to say?"

"I think she knows, Dan. Or at least, she's got a very good guess."

"How? I mean…is it Richard?"

"I think so. He stirred a hornet's nest by attacking that Inspector in Slough, and now he's gone and killed another person."

Daniel swore under his breath. "The police want to see me as well. I'm delaying it as much as I can."

"Don't avoid them for too long. They'll get suspicious. This DCI Baker has been to see Richard, as well."

"What did she tell you?"

Cora closed her eyes and leaned her head against the cold cement wall. The summer breeze filtered down from the trees, lifting her hair. Nothing touched the dark anxiety inside, pulling at her guts like a relentless tide.

"She talked about how Rachel was tortured. And there were other women as well. Dan, the cops know. And they won't let this go."

Daniel was silent for a few seconds. "Did she mention any names?"

"She knows Richard, and she mentioned you and Chris."

"Damn. Have you tried to contact Chris?"

"Yes. He's not answering his phone. I'm going to tell mum to speak to him."

"Good idea. I'll talk to her as well, and try his phone. Hold on tight, okay? The cops are just trying to scare you. They can't pin this on anyone, they're still fishing."

“I’d say their nets getting bloody close. We need to sort this out.”

“Don’t do anything rash. There’s nothing in the media as yet. I’m going to speak to my PR guy. Even if any news leaks out, we can put a spin on it through a press release.”

Cora hung up, and as she looked around the rear car park, she noticed a woman standing behind her car, observing the rear entrance discreetly. Her eyes met Cora’s, and she retreated into the portico.

When she peeked out, she saw Arla Baker striding up to the woman. Cora hung back again, her heart cannon balling against her ribs. She heard the engine, and then a car drove out. Cora looked out again, just in time to see the two detectives drive out. Arla Baker was looking out the passenger window. Cora jerked her head back instantly. She went inside. Her close protection officer, Adam, was standing next to her desk, an inquisitive expression on his face.

“Are you okay, ma’am?”

Cora ran a hand down her jacket. “Yes, I’m fine. Ask them to get me a cup of tea, please. Then I’ll see the people who’re waiting.”

Cora had no choice. She had to meet her constituents, this close to the election. But her mind flickered in and out, the past shining a torch into crevices of her mind, like a scuba diver descending into the trenches of the deepest ocean.

Between seeing people Cora sent out texts to Melissa and Julia, asking them to meet with her. An hour later, when she'd finished, she called Melissa, who answered.

"Meet me at the Astor Park Club in Chelsea, in half an hour." Astor Park was a member's only club, and they could talk discreetly there.

"I have clients-

Cora interrupted harshly. "This cannot wait. Say my name at the reception. They will show you in."

****

Astor Park Club lay on a quiet side street near Sloane Square. It occupied an entire corner of the street, but the magnificent, red and brown brick Victorian building was otherwise discreet. Only a small bronze plaque at the door proclaimed its name. Inside however, it was a different story.

The onyx marble floor reflected crystal chandeliers that hung low from the ceiling. Deep leather upholstery matched the soft carpet in the main rooms. It was so quiet even whispers could be heard. The street facing curtains were drawn, and the muted lights maintained the hushed atmosphere. Astor Park Club offered its exclusive members privacy and luxury, and no one could be a member without a recommendation from the board, and a thorough vetting process.

A woman showed Melissa and Julia into the main lounge, where Cora was sipping from a tumbler of rum. She was sat in a corner, shaded by an indoor palm tree. There was no one within eavesdropping distance.

Cora offered them a drink, and they ordered. Then Cora told them about Arla's visit.

"Have either of you told the police anything about Chris, or us?"

Melissa shook her head emphatically. "No. They asked, but I denied all knowledge."

Cora turned her piercing gaze to Julia. "What about you?"

Julia was white as a sheet, and her body trembled. Cora narrowed her eyes. "What's the matter?"

Their drinks arrived, and they waited till she had left.

Julia took a long gulp of her gin and tonic, draining half the glass. She breathed heavily. "Chris paid me a visit."

"What?" Cora frowned. "When?"

"Yesterday." Julia's eyes remained on the tabletop. A shaking hand reached up to tuck an errant strand behind her ear. Slowly, she raised her head and stared at Cora.

"He was…forceful. He hurt me. He wanted Kate's details. I wouldn't give it to him, so he turned…

"Violent?" Melissa asked.

"Yes. I gave him Kate's details. I had no choice."

"Did anyone see you and Chris together?" Cora asked.

"No. It was outside Bexley Heath, in a quiet street. It was just us."

"We need to keep a low profile," Cora said. "If the police ask to see you again, make an excuse, say you're busy. And don't speak to them without a solicitor." She glanced at Melissa, who nodded. But Julia worried her. Her face was ashen, and she looked on the brink of tears.

Julia wiped her eyes. "Hasn't this gone far enough? I think we need to tell the police what we know. I think they're going to find out-

"No, they won't," Cora put her elbows on the table and leaned forward. She kept her voice low. "Have you forgotten how much I've helped your careers? Without me, or my family's connections, you wouldn't be where you are today. Don't forget that."

She slid her eyes to Melissa, whose eyes were wide with fear, mouth open. She looked back at Julia, who cradled her head on her hand.

“Look at me,” She hissed at Julia. When she didn’t obey, Cora gripped her hand and shook it.

“If this gets out, then we’re all going down. Do you understand?”

Julia sniffed, and shook her head. “Kate was right. We should’ve come clean years ago. Now look what’s happened.” She locked troubled eyes with Cora. “How can we live like this?”

CHAPTER 41

Major Incident Room 1, or MIR1 as it was better known, was full to the brim. Arla was at the podium, the projector screen behind her.

It showed an image of the triangle she had drawn on her phone, from Islington to Hampstead Heath.

"We have three PCN's that report the same method of torture inflicted on the victims that Simon Barnaby alleges Rachel suffered from. The description of the man is the same in all the PCN's. This man was young back in 1998 or 2000 but he should be in his fifties now.

Arla pressed on the remote, and a E-fit face photo of a tall, slim, clean shaven man with glasses, popped up on the screen.

"The image has been sent out, so check the Met website and download to your phones. Be vigilant about this man. He is dangerous. We have a pool of suspects, but he might not be external to that pool."

Arla flicked another button, and photos of Richard McPherson, Daniel and Chris Underwood appeared on the screen. Arla related who they were.

"We have to be careful how we approach these men. Surveillance has started, and we will monitor them, but we cannot find Chris Underwood as yet."

Rob raised a hand from the front row. "We have CCTV sightings of Cora Underwood entering and leaving that house in Kensington Gore. There's no doubt she lives there.

"And that also means she, or someone else in that house, called Rachel's friends," Arla said. She moved to a new screen that showed Melissa, Julia and Kate.

"Do we have these three under surveillance?"

Rob said, "Apart from Kate, yes. Melissa and Julia are in London, so its easier. For Kate we have to request the Kent Constabulary, and they will start the process later tonight, or tomorrow."

The meeting broke up. Rob and Lisa hurried up to Arla. Lisa said, "We found one of the women who filed a PCN. She's the one who escaped from the man's car. She now lives in Tottenham, in the east end. Gita and Ros have gone to visit her."

"What about the other two?"

"One of them has died, and the other has agreed to attend the station. She should be here any minute."

"Good, I want to see her when she arrives."

Arla was tired and getting a headache. She had skipped lunch, and it was almost six pm now. Dinner time. Coffee and biscuits weren't her idea of a healthy meal, but she didn't have time for anything else. When she got to the office, she saw Harry. Her heart leapt with joy, but she also knew he was still on leave. He didn't have the head bandage anymore, and he looked like his usual self. Dressed like a banker in a flawless navy blue suit, shoes polished so hard he could probably see his own face in them.

He turned as Arla approached. "Sorry I missed the MIR meeting."

Arla pointed a finger at him. "You should be at home. Still two days left of your leave."

"Duty calls," Harry raised his eyebrows. Arla could smell his aftershave. Harry was back in business. She supressed a smile, and glanced at Greg, who was watching.

"Have you two met?"

"Yes," Greg said. "We were just chatting about Brian Copeland. He was one of our assets of course, but DI Mehta helped us get hold of him." He shook his head. "We should catch his killer soon. The CCTV data is getting checked as we speak."

Arla beckoned at Harry. "In my room for a debrief please."

Harry joined her and closed the door. Arla bought Harry up to date about her meeting with Cora.

“It’s one of her family members,” Arla said. “I’m convinced now, that’s why I called the MIR meeting. Daniel Underwood is still avoiding us and Chris is not answering his phone.”

“Are they your main suspects now? Along with McPherson.”

“Yes. We’ve taken swab samples from Cora and McPherson, and they weren’t happy about that. But if it shows a match anywhere that will be interesting.”

Harry said, “I wanted to check something. Do you have ID photos for Chris and Daniel? Do they match the e-fit?”

Arla opened her laptop and clicked on the images. She suppressed a yawn. It was time for dinner, and she was running on coffee and adrenaline. She didn’t feel hungry. An intimation of danger was gnawing at her guts. The killer was hiding in the shadows, waiting to make his next move.

Harry stood next to her as they examined the e-fit image. A simple, innocent looking man stared back at them. His cheeks were lean, sallow even, with a light beard. He had a sharp nose, and the glasses rested on them. He looked like a school teacher, or an academic. Perhaps an accountant. Someone who lived next door to you, and you said hi every morning if you came across him. Arla shuddered. The worst of mankind lived perfectly normal lives. No one suspected them.

Arla switched screens, and placed the photos of Daniel, Chris and McPherson next to the e-fit image. Daniel was stocky and swarthy, his cheeks puffy with a bull dog appearance. They had a photo of a younger McPherson from his first arrest, about twenty years ago. He did have a lean, suave look, but he still didn't match the e-fit.

When Chris's face appeared on the screen, Arla felt a trembling in her spine, that spread to her hands. For all three men, the photos had been from old passports and police records. Chris's photos belonged to his passport and driving licence, from 2003. He had a light brown beard, a beaked nose, and behind thin framed glasses, the studious, calm look of a man at peace with himself. But the blue eyes were like ice, cold and utterly devoid of emotion.

"Bingo," Harry whispered behind her.

CHAPTER 42

Kate shut her laptop and massaged her forehead. She had a splitting headache, and a pressure behind her eyes. She heard voices and opened her eyes. She was in her office, and she noticed two of her colleagues' stare at her and whisper to each other. Or was she being paranoid?

Kate got up, and shoved the laptop in her bag, then collected her things. It was five pm, and people were leaving. She cast a wary glance towards Jeff's office, and found it empty. She heaved a sigh of relief. She sneaked out before Jeff could collar her again.

At the reception lobby, she checked her phone once. No calls from Julia. Good. She didn't want to hear from her again, and nor from that bitch, Melissa. All Melissa cared for was her career.

Memories of that night swam into her memory, like a distant star. The star turned into a black hole, sucking the light and air out of the universe. Screams of anguish filled her mind, and the horror suddenly rooted her to the ground.

How could she not have done anything? She tried…but it wasn't good enough, was it? The guilt ate away inside her all these years, and now the horror was back.

"Kate?"

She came back to life, taking a deep breath as if she'd been underwater, and just broke free. She gasped softly and turned. Her boss, Jeff, was standing there, looking at her strangely.

"Are you alright?"

Kate brushed a hand over her ponytail and forced her lips to stretch into a smile.

"Yes, yes, I'm fine. How're you?"

Jeff continued his examination, and she fidgeted, trying to smile again but failing.

"It's just that since that call from the police you've been…distracted."

"Oh, that." Kate waved a hand in the air. "That was just about an old friend. She's fine now." She lied. Normally, when she tried flirt mode, it worked on Jeff. She knew he didn't have a girlfriend. She didn't take it too far, but her womanly wiles worked on Jeff. Not today, though. He was staring at her like a scientist gazing at bacteria on a Petri dish.

"Are you sure? I can get Anika to cover for you for a couple of days, if you want."

Anika had recently joined, a twenty-three-year-old university graduate. She was super keen, and Kate suspected she had her eye on Kate's job.

"No thanks," she said quickly. She fought to make the smile broader, and relaxed her body. "I'm fine, honestly. I was just tired from not sleeping well. Think I need to head back to the gym again."

Jeff looked uncertain. "As long as you're sure."

"Yes I am."

Jeff walked out, and she heaved a sigh of relief. She waited for him to reach the end of the complex and then walk out the gates. Then she walked out herself, making sure Jeff, or any of her colleagues, weren't around to see her. She did have friends in the office. Catherine and Debbie – two women her age, and she bonded well with them. But they worked three days a week, and Debbie was in finance.

Kate checked her phone as she walked to the bus stop. She had a new message from Catherine, asking if she was free over the weekend. In fact, Kate wanted to get out of Broadstairs for a while. It was nice being here, but it was also a small town. Kate needed a holiday, and she wanted to get a plane ticket to Thailand and just bloody leave for a couple of weeks. She loved that about being single, and not having any ties, apart from her parents who lived in the Wirral…

And just like that, Chris's words returned, tarnishing her mind. The sunlight turned to rust, the rot spread inside her chest. She shook her head as the streets slipped past, invisible to her eyes now. The summer sun was still present, and it would be for the next couple of hours, till eight or nine pm. But it had turned night for her already, the anxiety of Chris's words nibbling at the depths of her soul.

Kate lived in the ground floor of a Victorian conversion. The terraced houses were wide and spacious, and the two-bed conversion was plenty of space for her, and she got the garden. She went in and shut the door, the locked it behind her. Her eyes scanned the living room to the left, and the open plan kitchen area to the right. Everything was in its place.

She went to the bedrooms and bathrooms. No gremlins in there. The patio door from the second bedroom was locked, curtains drawn. Everything was as she had left it in the morning. She told herself she was being silly. She drank a glass of water at the kitchen filter tap, and exhaled. There was nothing like coming home, was there? She could put her feet up for a while now.

She had a message from Debbie, asking about the weekend as well. Why not? She hadn't been out with them for almost three weeks. They met up once a month. She agreed on their group chat called *Broadstairs Bitches.*

She made herself a cup of tea, and flopped on the sofa. She called her mother, and her eyes closed with relief when she heard her voice.

“We’re fine, dear. Weather’s nice, and the wind died down today. Lovely view across the valley.”

“Good. How’s dad?”

“His left knee’s giving him trouble but apart from that he’s fine.”

They chatted for a while, then Kate said goodbye. She checked the time. Almost seven pm. She wanted to open yesterdays bottle of wine. But no, she should make an effort. Haul her sorry arse to the gym. That helped with her mood, and her demons.

She went to her bedroom to get changed. As she was pulling on her sports bra, she heard a sound outside. A floorboard squeaking. Kate froze. She listened intently. The house was quiet. A pipe gurgled somewhere then went quiet. There was no sound. Had she imagined it?

A door creaked somewhere. Outside, in the hallway. Panic mushroomed in her belly, but she told herself not to panic. Again, she was being silly. Her nerves were on edge after that idiot had called. But there was no one here. He didn’t know where she lived, anyway. The whole thing was just…stupid.

Kate looked around for her phone. It wasn’t on the bed, or on the bedside tables. She got dressed, listening for sounds. There was none. Satisfied, she opened the door and went out in the hallway. The bathroom door was half open, and she was sure she shut it. Frowning, she looked inside. The bathroom was empty. She went to the kitchen, and looked for her phone. It wasn't on the sofa, or the kitchen counter.

Then she heard the floorboard creak again. It came from behind her, in the hallway. It sounded again.

This time, hairs stood up in the back of her neck, and sudden fear flooded her limbs. She felt a presence behind her.

She whirled around. A man was standing there. Tall, thin, with a black denim jacket and jeans. He had a light beard on his face, and the same black frame glasses on his eyes that gave him a studious, nerdy look. She recognised him immediately.

Chris Underwood.

He smiled, and held up her phone. "Looking for this?"

Panic had claimed her brain, words frozen on her tongue. Her heart slammed against her ribs like stormy waves on rocks. She couldn't breathe.

He didn't move. He stood there, with that almost gentle smile on his face, while his eyes remained cold, like a shark's dead stare on its prey.

Kate's hands were claws on her sides, fists jammed hard on her jogging tights. "How…how…

"Your patio door lock's not very hard to pick. You need to get that checked. When I heard you come in, I hid under the bed in the guest room."

Through the fog of fear that was overcoming her, Kate stepped back, towards the front door. Chris followed her, his eyes wary now.

"You need to leave now," she whispered. "Or I'm going to –

"Call the police?" He held out her phone. "Here, take it."

Kate grit her teeth together. "Put my phone down. And leave."

"I just want to talk." His smile faltered. "What did you tell the police?"

"Get out!" Kate shouted, pointing at the door. He had stepped closer. He lunged for her suddenly, and the speed of his movement surprised. He was lean and strong, but she screamed and fought. He clasped a hand around her mouth, smothering her voice. Kate felt her head slammed against the tiles, and pain exploded in her skull. Her eyes rocked and her head hit the hard tiles again. She couldn't speak, and her body went limp, then her world went totally

CHAPTER 43

"You think this is going to work?" Harry asked, staring out of the windscreen. They were parked outside number 6 Kensington Gore. It was a sumptuous detached, red brick building. Iron grill gates, and a red brick wall that reached several metres into the sky barricaded the front. The house was visible through the grill gate. Ivy grew over the front wall, pink flowers in bloom. Kensington Gore was one of the loveliest residential spots in London, built in the eighteenth century for the newly wealthy Victorian merchants. Old world charm oozed from every brick in the secluded, hushed street.

Arla murmured from the passenger seat. "Something has to work. Did Rob feedback anything?"

Rob and Lisa had gone to Daniel Underwood's office. "Not yet," Harry said, looking at his phone.

"Here we go," Arla said. A black Range Rover pulled up in front of the house. The gates started to slide open. Arla opened the door and ran across the street. Harry followed. The car swept in through the gates, and so did Arla and Harry. A guard approached them, holding out an arm.

"I'm sorry, you can't be here."

Arla sized him up. She could tell from his buzz cut and athletic build he was ex-Army. But he didn't have a weapon, or at least one that was visible. Arla ignored him, and pulled on the passenger door. It opened, and a shocked Cora Underwood stared back at her.

"Miss Underwood. We need to speak urgently."

The Close Protection Officer (CPO) was at Arla's shoulder, and Harry was holding him back. Arla didn't want a physical fight, but the situation was rapidly getting out of control.

"We know what your brother did," Arla said. "He's been killing women for the last three decades. It's time he stopped."

Arla might as well have reached inside the car and slapped Cora across the face. Cora's eyes popped wider, and her jaws relaxed.

Next to Arla, Harry and Adam, Cora's CPO, had got into a tussle. The guard had also joined in.

"If you don't tell me where Chris is right now, I have no choice but to arrest you," Arla said. "That will be a public record, and anyone can access it. Is that what you want?"

Cora hesitated. Arla turned back, and tried to stop the tussle between Harry and the two men. They had put Harry against the car and Adam was drawing his gun. Arla didn't hesitate. She took out her extendable steel baton, flicked it to the full height, and slammed it down on Adam's gun arm. He yelped in pain, and the gun fell to the floor.

Arla pulled out her radio with her other hand. "I'm calling for assistance now, and you're under arrest for assaulting a police officer."

"Stop!" Cora cried out. She had stepped out of the car. She held up both hands, and moved behind Arla to push the guard back. Adam stumbled backwards, and fell on the gravel drive. He stood up quickly, cursing and holding his injured arm. He glared at Arla.

Arla ignored him and whipped around to face Cora. She had the radio turned on to receive, and thrust it in Cora's face.

"Shall I call for assistance? Do you want this place to become a crime scene?"

"Turn the radio off," Cora said, her chest heaving, blotches of crimson on her cheeks. "And come inside."

She stalked off, heading for the yellow stone porch. Inside it, a brown wooden door was visible. Cora pressed a fob key on the side wall, and the door swung open. Harry stood next to Arla.

"You okay?" She asked.

"I'm fine," he looked warily at Adam and the other guard, who were now flanking them. "Let's go."

Harry led Arla inside. She still clutched the steel baton, but flicked it down, and then put it back on her waist belt as they entered the property.

The reception area was all dark panelled wood, and parquet flooring, like she'd expected. Cora was standing there, and she pointed to a room on the left. Arla followed her. They stepped inside, and Cora shut the door behind them.

It was a study, with a large mahogany desk in the middle, facing the bay windows. Cora sat behind the desk. Arla and Harry pulled up chair. As she did so, Arla's eye fell on a brochure. It had a glossy black cover, with the logo of Underwood Property Group on it. It was a collection of circles, all blending into one another. Breath hitched in Arla's chest as she recognised the logo.

She pointed to it, and looked at Carla. "Did the Underwood Group make clothes?"

Cora frowned. She took her time, as if trying to consider the motive behind Arla's question, then nodded.

"Yes, we had a retail clothing business. It didn't last. We folded it up many years ago. Why?"

"Clothes with that logo were found in Rachel Mathew's possession. And on her skeleton."

Cora remained silent. Harry took out the e-fit photo from his coat pocket and slid it across the table to

Cora. She glanced at it, and colour drained from her face.

"That's your brother, Chris, isn't it?" Arla asked. Cora raised her head slowly. It seemed she had a sock in her mouth. Her lips parted, but she couldn't speak.

Arla said, "We got that e-fit photo from the descriptions of the victims who managed to escape from Chris. Other women were not so lucky. I know if we search through Hampstead Heath, we will find more human remains like Rachel's."

Arla stood, and walked to the table. She put her hands on the top, and leaned forward. "We're going after Chris, and you can't stop us anymore. Your gangster Uncle can't. The bent cops in your pay, and your political connections can't either. And soon, this will be all over the papers. It will be the end of your political career."

Cora seemed to have difficulty breathing. She shrank back on the chair. For the first time, she looked scared, even helpless.

"But I can help you," Arla said. "We don't have to do a press conference or a media coverage, if you tell us where he is. This doesn't have to hit the papers, and get you and your family's name on it. So tell us where he is."

"I don't know," Cora whispered, her voice cracked and broken. "But I can give you his phone number."

"When did you last see him?" Harry asked.

"We don't meet often. I asked my mother. She hasn't seen him either."

"Give me his phone number." Harry took the number and stepped outside to call the team to alert them. They could triangulate calls from that number, and hopefully, get a location hook on Chris.

Arla focused on Cora. "Julia and Melissa aren't answering my calls. Why?"

Cora was slumped on her chair, and cradled her head in her hands. "I met with them. Told them not to engage with you."

"Does your brother Daniel know where Chris might be? Or Richard Mcpherson?"

"Daniel doesn't know. I don't know about Richard."

"Why, Cora?" Arla shook her head. "All these years, you protected a monster."

Cora didn't answer. Arla said, "You knew Rachel, didn't you? You were the unknown friend the neighbour's saw. And when the DNA reports become available tomorrow, we will get a match with your and Chris's DNA, won't we?"

Cora looked to one side, not answering Arla. But her silence was all the admission Arla needed. The door opened and Harry burst in. He held up his radio.

“Last signal from Chris’s phone triangulated to Broadstairs, in Kent. Traffic are checking the address as they speak.”

“That’s where Kate Turner lives,” Arla said. She whipped her eyes to Cora. “Do you know anything about this? Did you tell Chris where Kate lives?”

Cora gripped her forehead. “No. But Julia did.”

CHAPTER 44

Light was fading from the sky as Harry drove the black BMW. The car hurtled down the motorway towards Broadstairs. Clouds had darkened the horizon, and drops of rain appeared on the windscreen, setting the wipers in motion. Arla held on for dear life as Harry swerved past a truck at high speed, and then overtook a couple of cars in the fast lane. The four litre, sixteen valve engine whined and growled, and the car leapt forward.

Arla's radio crackled and she answered. "DCI Baker."

"Inspector Wasim from the Kent Constabulary. Your suspect is not located. Neither is the victim. Her house is empty, and the front door unlocked. There are signs of a struggle in the kitchen."

"He's abducted her," Arla raised her voice above the engine. "Have you spoken to the neighbours? Checked CCTV?"

Arla heard a babble of voices on the radio, and she held on. Wasim returned on the line.

"A neighbour saw a man in the garden. He came in over the rear fence. This happened around three PM."

"That will be our suspect, Chris Underwood. What else did the neighbour see?"

The line faded and then the radio came back to life. "…called 999. They went through the rear door in the fence."

"Sorry you cut out there," Arla shouted.

"The suspect and victim went through a gate that leads out from the rear garden, into the street beyond. The neighbour had called 999 when she saw that."

"Good, anything on CCTV? This man is highly dangerous. We need to catch him without delay. The suspect's life is at risk."

"Will get back to you as soon as we have visual."

The line went dead. Harry's face was a mask of concentration as he gripped the steering wheel tightly. Kent was a large county, and a lot of it hugged the south east coast of England. Its beaches, and resort towns were well known. Arla flicked open the map on her phone, and checked Kate's address again. They were still an hour away.

"We need to speed up," Arla said. Harry nodded without answering. Arla's head hit the back of the seat as Harry floored the pedal. The car zoomed ahead like a nuclear arrow on the line of black asphalt. The clouds were thicker, and the rain continued to splatter, but it wasn't a downpour, so Harry's vision wasn't compromised.

Arla called Lisa. "Arrest Richard McPherson and Mike Boland. If they resist, charge them with suspects to murder."

"Okay guv."

"Have we set up surveillance on Julia and Melissa?"

"Yes, guv. They're not still answering their phones, but both of them are at home, and we have squad cars parked outside. CCTV on their streets is active on our feeds. No one will get close to them without our knowing."

"Good. Has Greg Warren got the CCTV footage of Copeland's killer?"

"Let me call him to check. I'll give you a bell back."

Countless minutes passed, but finally they took the exit for Broadstairs. Arla's radio chirped as Harry slowed down in the town traffic.

"Wasim speaking. Suspects vehicle is a navy-blue Audi A3, and he was seen driving towards the cliffs over Darwin Bay. There's no CCTV on the cliffs, but we are headed that way."

“Joining you there,” Arla looked at Harry and he nodded without taking his eyes off the road. Wasim’s voice was coming over on the dashboard loudspeaker.

Harry entered the location key Wasim provided, and he put his siren on. The cars ahead parted reluctantly. Arla wound the window down. The air smelt of the sea and a gust of wind blew inside the car, ruffling her hair. The rain was pelting down now, smudging the red lights of cars in front.

Harry swerved and turned, then took a sharp right, tyres squealing, cars braking within inches of the BMW’s bonnet. Arla was thrust forward and back like a rag doll, even with the seat belt on. Then Harry sped up, heading for Darwin’s Bay.

CHAPTER 45

The dirt track appeared in the headlights, veering off from the narrow road that led into the cliffs. On the dashboard, they saw the sat nav indicating nothing but a dark mass ahead, which meant barely any coverage. The land shrugged into giant boulders around them, and the track sloped upwards into the hills. The air was colder here, and the rain drummed on the windscreen, making the wipers work furiously.

Arla called Wasim on the radio. "ETA seventeen minutes according to the location you sent me. But we have no sat nav any more. Do we just follow the road?"

"Yes," Wasim said. "There's no other way, unless you want to walk."

"Have you called for air support? We need a helicopter in case the victim falls on a cliff ledge."

"Positive. Air Support enroute, scrambled from Tunbridge Wells air base. Twenty minutes ETA."

Arla hung up as the car bounced along the dirt track. They hit a hole on the road and then slammed against a bump. Arla banged her head against the window.

"Ouch," she shouted. "Harry, watch it."

"Do you want to drive?" Harry grimaced. "I can barely see where I'm going. Bloody rain had to pick up now."

The track was turning into slush, streams of water running down past the car. The headlights showed the driving rain forming pools of water, hiding the cracks and holes on the path. Harry was forced to slow down, turning the wheel savagely to avoid craters on the road.

Finally, they saw the flashing blue lights ahead. The going was still frustratingly slow. Arla unbuckled her belt when they were within walking distance. They ditched the car, and tried to run across the grassland. The smell of heather and gorse hung heavy in the air, their smell held captive in the humid, rainy air. Arla's feet sank in the soft ground, and she had to accept Harry's help.

A torchlight flashed in their direction, and a tall man in a high vis uniform appeared. He was wearing wellies, Arla noted, and she wished they had a spare pair or two in the car.

"Inspector Wasim," the man shouted, shaking her rain wet hand. "Nice to meet you." He pointed at the flat earth running ahead, and his words were lost in the howl of the wind.

"What did you say?" Arla shouted back.

"He's over there," Wasim shouted in her ears. We found the car near the edge of the cliff. Two uniformed units are up there already. You can't drive up, it's on foot. We tried, and a car got stuck in the mud."

The wind screamed over the North Sea, and Arla had to listen closely to hear Wasim. They trudged over the mud and squelching wet earth, Arla's trousers now soaked up to her knees. Several times she almost fell over, and once she nearly pulled Harry down with her. But he was strong, and each time, got her out of the ground. Somehow, they managed to follow Wasim, who was having an easier time with his wellies.

Then they saw him. Chris was lit up by the torchlight of two uniformed officers, who stood a few metres away. He held Kate in his arms. She was flopping, barely conscious, hair cascading down her face.

"Don't come any closer," Chris shouted. He took a step backwards. The officers didn't move.

"Chris!" Arla shouted, coming forward. He heard her voice and looked in her direction.

"I'm DCI Baker. I spoke to your sister, Cora. She wants to see you."

"Ah, Arla Baker," Chris shouted. Arla was close to him now, no more than ten metres away. He said something else, but the wind drowned his words.

Arla shouted back. "Leave Kate, Chris. She's done nothing wrong."

He said something, which she didn't hear. Then he stepped back further, inching towards the cliff.

Arla followed, but Harry held her back. "No," Arla screamed. Then she saw Kate lift her head. She brushed the hair off her face and looked around. She was still drowsy, but her eyes picked up the lights, and seemed to understand what was happening. She struggled to get free but Chris still held her tight.

Arla's words were drowned out in the rotor wash of the helicopter, which zoomed in over their heads. It banked over the sea, and turned, it's headlight now focused on the back of Chris. His feet were getting dangerously close to the edge. With a sinking heart, Arla saw small rocks skittering off the edge of the cliff.

Then her eyes hooked with Kate. With wild eyes, she was staring at Arla. A silent communication passed between them. Arla nodded slowly, making sure Kate saw it. Chris was looking around him, and trying to see how close the helicopter was getting. Arla knew they wouldn't get too close to the cliff edge, for fear of crashing against it.

“Do it now, Kate,” Arla whispered, holding the woman’s eyes. Kate kicked at Chris’s legs as she fell to the floor, dragging him down. She was strong, and she caught Chris by surprise. The uniformed officers ran towards them, realising she was trying to get free. So did Arla and Harry.

But Chris recovered, stumbling backwards. He fell to his knees, but his arm remained hooked around Kate’s waist. He dragged her back, and they were now on the edge, the endless void down to the North Sea opening up behind them.

“No!” Arla screamed. She saw Kate’s mouth open, and fear morphing her face. Chris tugged on her again, and together, they vanished over the ledge, into the darkness.

CHAPTER 46

Arla and Harry rushed to the edge. The helicopter was directly overhead now, and the rotor wash was almost flattening them.

"Get down," Harry shouted in her ears, pulling her to the wet earth. Arla lay on her front and inched towards the edge. The rain was less, but the wet earth was slushy, and she was drenched within seconds. The search light from the helicopter zoomed down, lighting them up as Arla crawled to the edge, her heart empty with sorrow and disappointment. She couldn't stop Chris, and it was her fault.

She looked down and saw nothing but the beam of light getting sucked into the dark void below. Then she heard a shout from her left, and the beam of light moved. One of the uniform officers was pointing down, frantically. They saw a ledge, an outcropping of the cliff. A human figure lay there, crumpled, curled up into a foetal position. It was Kate.

The helicopter moved downwards, and the light beam was stronger. Kate stirred. Arla shouted, her voice hoarse, but the wind swallowed her words. The beam moved, and she saw a fearful sight.

Fingers, gripping the corner of the ledge. A man was dangling from the corner, his feet scrambling for purchase on the cliff edge. The helicopter swept down lower, and the rotor was now stronger, and Arla was forced to put her head down. But she could still see.

A face rose up from under the edge, tainted with pain and the effort. It was Chris. He tried to hook a hand over the edge, but he failed. The rotor wash shoved him backwards. Then his hands gave up the fight with gravity. They slipped, and hung on for an interminable second or two, then finally, vanished. The searchlight beam picked him up as he fell, arms cartwheeling, body flailing in the wind.

Then he was gone, merging into the endless black space like a shadow that had never existed.

One of the uniformed officers had descended onto the ledge. He had a rope tied around his waist, and his two colleagues on the cliff held on to the rope. Harry and Wasim joined them to assist.

Wasim was speaking to the pilot and his helper on the radio. Kate was conscious now. A rope dangled down from the helicopter. It was tied around Kate's waist. Then a ladder lowered, swaying wildly in the wind.

The officer on the ledge held Kate against him, and then tied the rope around their waists. He gripped the lowest rung of the ladder, then holding Kate, he stepped on the ladder, holding it tight with both hands.

The helicopter moved higher with both of them on the lowest rung of the ladder. The metallic bird moved over Arla's head, and roared over the cliff.

The bird deposited Kate and the officer on solid ground. Then the saviour pilot veered up higher, and left the scene.

Arla knelt next to Kate. She could barely speak, but words were not necessary. Arla folded Kate in her arms as the woman wept.

CHAPTER 47

Kate was admitted to the Royal Tunbridge Wells Hospital. Arla stood outside the door of her room, and spoke to the doctor.

"She's in shock, but she will make a full recovery."

"Yes, I've spoken to her. Thanks for your help."

Arla watched as the doctor went to the end of the ward, and outside into the main corridor.

"We should go home," Harry said. "We still have work to do."

"Yes," Arla agreed. She was exhausted, and her clothes were still wet. "Did Rob call you back?"

"Yes." Harry didn't look much better. His trousers and coat were soaked. "We should stop at a service station and buy some new clothes if we can."

"As long as Rob and the others are doing what we told them to."

"They are, so don't worry."

Arla took one last look at Kate through the window, then they left. It was past midnight, and they found a service station, but there was no clothes shop, as Arla had expected. They went back to the nick, where they kept a change of clothes in their lockers, like every police officer.

Everyone in the team had gone home, apart from Lisa and Rob. They stood when Arla and Harry walked in, holding cups of coffee.

Rob said, "Do you really want to do this now guv? We can wait till tomorrow morning."

Arla shook her head. "No. We need to finish this. Let's go."

They drove to Julia Slater's house. She was asleep, and not happy to see Arla.

"It's two in the morning. What do you want?"

"You're under arrest. You need to come with us to the station."

Arla turned and left, leaving a shell-shocked Julia staring after her. They repeated the process with Melissa.

At the nick, Arla sat them down in a meeting room. She faced Julia and Melissa, and neither of them were happy. Harry sat next to Arla.

"I'm a barrister," Melissa said. "I don't have to speak to you without a lawyer. I know my rights."

"Good," Arla said. "You can do whatever you want. But I need to tell you what I learnt from Kate Turner."

Melissa froze, and then the two women looked at each other.

Arla said, "Kate has carried a secret all these years. She wanted to come clean, but you two didn't let her. In fact," Arla pointed at Melissa, "You threatened her, with Cora's family's help. To save herself, Kate left London."

Melissa's lips tightened, her nostrils flared, but she remained silent.

Arla said, "Chris has just tried to kill Kate, in Broadstairs. We were just in time to stop him."

Julia gasped. "Is she okay?"

"She's fine. She's suffered a concussion and mild head trauma, but luckily nothing serious. She's in shock, but she's alright."

Arla looked at each woman in turn, and neither of them could hold her gaze. Then Melissa spoke.

"I want a lawyer."

"Very well, you can get the duty solicitor. But before that, let me tell you a little story."

She sipped her coffee. "Twenty-eight years ago, Rachel Mathews told Kate about how she was being physically abused by Chris Underwood. Kate told Julia, and also you, Melissa."

“But by that time, Melissa was already working with Cora Underwood. Cora was your mentor, wasn’t she?”

Melissa sat in stony silence, her baleful eyes glaring at Arla.

“So the three of you had a meeting. Melissa wanted to hush the whole thing up, but Kate didn’t want to. She said Rachel should go to the police. Julia – you agreed, but you were subdued by Melissa. How am I doing so far?”

Again, only silence radiated from the two women. Arla felt something else too – waves of guilt.

“Julia – Cora helped your career as well, didn’t she? That’s why you have that expensive clinic in Cadogan Square. You were marketed as a famous psychologist, even though you were junior. That money and publicity came from the Underwood family.”

“But Rachel’s abuse continued, and Kate kept telling her to go to the police. One night, things came to a head. The four of you met up by Regent’s Canal in a secluded spot. The canal side was then being developed by the Underwood Group. You met inside a newly constructed but empty building.”

Arla stopped. The two women had their eyes fixed on Arla, as if hypnotised.

“That night, Rachel broke down. She said she was going to the police. She left the meeting, running out on the canal towpath. Melissa, you tried to stop her. Rachel slipped and fell, her head hitting the cement on the towpath. She died."

Arla sat back and sighed, then drank more of her coffee. Her tiredness was like a giant forceps squeezing her brain. But she carried on.

"Kate wanted to call the cops. So did you, Julia. But Melissa – you found a tarpaulin sheet inside the construction site. You told the others to keep a secret. It was an accident. If you called the police, they would find out about Chris, and they would also suspect the three of you. Or at least, that's what you told them. Isn't that right, Melissa?"

Melissa glared at her.

Arla continued. "So you wrapped Rachel's body in the tarpaulin sheet, tied stones on it, and put the body in the canal water. It was dark, and the building had a back entrance on the tow path. No one was around. No one saw you."

Arla stopped and laned back in her chair.

Melissa said, "It's a good story, but you need proof, Inspector. How can you verify any of this?"

Harry spoke for the first time. "Because none of you wore gloves that night. You left fingerprints and DNA on the tarpaulin, and also hair follicles. The fingerprints are now damaged, but the DNA and hair remains."

Melissa became an iron statue, her face rigid like a mask. Julia looked like she had been punched in the guts.

Harry said, "The DNA match with your hair and skin cells should be back tomorrow. We called you tonight for two reasons. One, to place you under arrest so you don't try to escape. You could, with the help of the Underwood family. Two, to give you a chance to confess. As you know, that saves us a lot of time and effort with the Crown Prosecution Service (CPS). Confessing also gives you a shorter sentence."

He looked from Melissa to Julia. "The Underwood family, and Cora, don't want anything to do with you anymore. They want their name out of the court case. You're on your own."

He waited, letting that sink in. Melissa's lower lip trembled, and her face was ashen. She breathed heavily.

Julia whispered. "It's true." Melissa turned to her sharply, but Julia ignored her.

"Yes, we did it."

"Julia. Stop it!" Melissa shouted.

"Keep your voice down," Harry said. "Unless you want to go to a cell now."

Julia stared at the desk not raising her head. "It happened just like you said. Neither of us could take it anymore. The guilt was killing me. Then this happened, and it…I know it sounds awful, but it was an easy way out."

Arla said, "You could just tell everyone that Rachel was depressed, and hence vanished, maybe took an overdose and committed suicide."

Harry added, "And reporting her missing actually deflected suspicion from you. All of you cooperated with the police for the same reason."

"But Kate wasn't happy, and that's why you got the Underwood family to threaten her. She promised her silence, and then she went off to Kent."

Julia nodded in silence. Melissa was staring at her, aghast.

Arla said, "Julia Slater and Melissa Carrington, both of you are under arrest for the murder of Rachel Mathews."

CHAPTER 48

It was six in the morning, and Arla had a fitful four hours sleep. When the alarm bell woke her up, she slapped it shut, and promptly fell asleep again. Harry, for some reason, was bright and cheerful. He shook her awake and practically lifted her out of bed.

"Come on sleepyhead." He held her upright, and looked into her eyes. "Unless you want to stay, and I can handle this. There will be back up, so don't worry."

"No," Arla straightened, brushing hair from her face. "I want to do this." She went to the bathroom and got ready quickly. Hair in a ponytail, and no make up. She looked like she'd been dragged through cactus plants, and felt like it, too. But she was almost at the end, and she couldn't stop now.

Harry drove them to the station, and the streets were quiet, south west London's residents still either in bed, or waking up. At Clapham Common nick, a squad car was waiting for them. Once Harry and Arla were in, the constable driving turned the flashing blues and sirens on. They sped through the deserted streets, heading for a place in North London called Wood Green.

Arla clutched a plastic cup of coffee, and took long sips. She glanced at Harry, and saw him take out a gun from his pocket. Her heart skipped a beat, but not in a nice way. Alarm spread through her body, but she had expected this. She knew nothing about guns, and had no idea what make or model the weapon was, apart from that it looked modern and slick.

It was strange, seeing a gun in Harry's hand. He had to keep it at the station, he wasn't allowed to take it home. AFO's (authorised firearms officer) had strict rules on what they could do with their weapons.

Harry caught her watching. "It's a Glock 22," he said. He pressed a button, and the magazine fell out. He counted the rounds, then slapped the magazine back in.

"Is the safety catch on?" Arla asked in a small voice.

Harry grinned. "Yes, silly." He checked a few things, then put the weapon back in his pocket. Well, what will be, will be, Arla thought to herself. She put her head back on the head rest and closed her eyes.

She didn't sleep, and listened to the radio chatter, updating her on the situation. In half an hour, they arrived at their destination. The residential street of modest, terraced houses was just waking up, a few yellow rectangles and squares appearing on the windows.

"All units in position," Arla's radio crackled. "Suspect still in the house."

"This is Gold Command," Arla said on the radio. "DCI Baker."

The three units in surveillance chimed in. Arla had worked hard to get Johnson to agree to this. Gold Command was the highest police command in London, and for two hours today, Arla had the power to veto any other police operation. She didn't feel any elation. Only disappointment at what she had to do, and a weariness that weighed down her bones.

She walked up to the house and knocked on the door. A light went on inside, and then Greg Warren appeared, in his bathrobe. He looked astonished to see Arla, and then Harry.

"Bit early, isn't it?" Greg wiped a hand across his jaw. "What are you doing here?"

"There was a new development in the case I need to tell you about. It can't wait."

"Oh?"

"Can we come in?"

"Of course." Greg moved to one side, and they stepped inside. He shut the door, then led them down the narrow hallway to the living room at the end, next to the small kitchen. The place was clean and well built, and Arla knew Greg lived alone.

“Do you mind if I get changed?” Greg smiled. “I just got out of the shower.”

“Have a seat,” Arla said. “This won’t take long.”

Greg still maintained his surprise, but Arla could see his mind working, thinking about the options. He sat down. So did Arla, but Harry remained standing, by the door. Greg turned to look at him once. Slowly, he turned back to Arla. He was relaxed, but his hands moved on his lap.

Arla said, “Many years ago, you were a uniformed constable at the Paddington Green nick. 1995, I believe.”

“Yes,” Greg shrugged. “Gosh, that takes me way back.” His manner was easy, inquisitive. He had a certain charisma, and that had helped him, all these years.

“You met a detective inspector there called Brian Dempsey. He became your mentor. He encouraged you to become a detective.”

Greg blinked a few times. He spoke slowly, as if he was aware of what Arla was trying to get at.

“Yes. And I know that Brian was later checked by the ACU. That had nothing to do with me. It happened several years later.”

“And you were also good friends with Sergeant Mike Boland.”

"Many years ago, yes. How is this relevant?"

Arla changed tack. "Where were you the night Brian Copeland was killed?"

Greg frowned. "I was at the Clapham nick, with you. Then I left, and checked in with DI Sanderson at the Cricklewood nick. They were gathering CCTV footage from the Greyfriars Estate. Then I came home."

"Only the CCTV didn't show anything, did it? The killer knew how to avoid the cameras. But the killer messed up in two areas. One, when I was at the crime scene, he told me there was no exit wound on Brian's skull. Hence, the bullet did not mark the wall."

Greg opened his mouth to speak, but Arla raised her hand, silencing him.

"But the pathologist reported late last night there *was* an exit wound from the skull. And there was a bullet mark on the wall. Only, it was covered up with a touch of paint. Forensics found it, and they have confirmed it was from a bullet."

Greg was shaking his head. "Arla, I really don't understand what you're trying to say."

"I'm saying you didn't go home that night. You found out from your boss, McPherson, exactly where Brian Copeland was. You knew him, of course, and it was you who warned Mcpherson that we were going to Slough to interview Brian. Hence, we were attacked there. The night he died, you called him, and he was expecting you."

Arla paused. Greg was breathing heavily, his eyes fixed on her.

Arla continued. "That's why there's no sign of breaking and entry in the flat where Brian was killed. You went in, then shot him from behind. The bullet made an exit wound which you covered up. Then you took the bullet and cartridge, and left."

Greg frowned, and stood up. His mouth moved, and his eyes flashed. "This is preposterous. Apart from being totally false, you also have no proof of this." He moved his hands like an aggrieved victim. "Not that there would be any proof, because I didn't bloody do it."

"Yes, we have proof. You avoided the CCTV, but you didn't factor in a dashcam on a driver's window on the street. That camera feed shows the street, and the exit of the building. It shows you leaving the building at three in the morning."

Greg was slowly turning the colour of the white washed walls. His mouth made a sucking sound, like a fish out of water.

"I…I think you're mistaken. The camera shows someone else."

Arla shook her head. "No, facial recognition proves its you. You are the reason McPherson always had vital witnesses silenced at his court trials. They were either bribed, or killed. As a Special Branch Inspector, you had access to the most classified information. You even caried out surveillance on your own boss, while informing him about it all along."

"I don't have to listen to this." Greg whirled around, and stopped abruptly. Harry was at the door, pointing his gun at him.

Harry spoke softly. "Sit down, Greg. There's no escape. The rear garden is blocked. There's a unit outside your front door."

"Sit down," Harry repeated, stepping forward. His eyes scanned the pockets of Greg's dressing gown. No bulge of a weapon there. Greg breathed hard, but sat down. His teeth ground together as he faced Arla.

Arla said, "We checked your passport. You travel a lot. South America – Belize in particular. And Malaga. We're waiting on data from Interpol, but Spanish police know a man who matches your appearance, but has a different passport. You've been spotted in Malaga with your boss, Richard McPherson. He's got a nice villa on the beach, hasn't he?"

Greg was staring at Arla, looking like he'd seen a ghost.

Arla said, "Ballistics will confirm the bullet came from a gun you own. There's at least two car dashcams that saw you, and also CCTV on the street as you drove away. You will be convicted for Brian Copeland's death."

Harry spoke on his radio. He kept his gun trained on Greg, while Arla opened the door for two uniformed officers.

They handcuffed Greg. Arla stood in front of him. "Greg Warren, you are under arrest for the murder of Brian Copeland. Also for aiding and abetting a known criminal, and involvement in organised crime."

Arla nodded to the uniforms, who took Greg away. She followed Harry out into the street. As she watched Greg put in the back seat of the squad car, she felt an immense exhaustion claim her limbs, a bone crushing tiredness that made her feel dizzy.

"Let's go home," she whispered to Harry.

THE END

Printed in Great Britain
by Amazon

60475000R00194